the driftless zone

the driftless zone

or a novel concerning the selective outmigration from small cities

by Rick Harsch

STEERFORTH PRESS

SOUTH ROYALTON, VERMONT

For information about permission to reproduce
selections from this book, write to:
Steerforth Press L.C., P.O. Box 70, South Royalton, Vermont 05068.

Library of Congress Cataloging-in-Publication Data
Harsch, Rick, 1959 –
The driftless zone, or, A novel concerning the selective outmigration from small
cities / by Rick Harsch. — 1st ed.
p. cm.
ISBN 1-883642-32-9 (alk. paper)
I. Title.
PS3558.A67557D75   1997
813' .54 — dc21   97-6420
CIP

Though it's true that none of the characters or events herein have been drawn
from real life — the people are inventions and they never did these things — it's
equally true that I regret having endured anyone or any incident resembling them.

— R.H.

The text of this book was composed by Steerforth Press using a
digital version of Sabon.

Manufactured in the United States of America

FIRST PAPERBACK EDITION

For Michael Welch, who paid for it, and Tom Kneifl, Bill Pemberton, Jim Lafky, Daisy, Prasenjit Gupta, Jack Harsch, Ellie Harsch, Dick Mial, Jim McPherson, and in memory of Bill Vettes, who once at age 72 made solid contact on 143 of 144 80 mph fastballs, the one he missed low and a foot outside though he swung anyway and said "shit" when he missed

Chapter One is for Sesshu Foster
Chapter Three is for Adam Snyder
Spleen is for Marc Wehrs
Several specific phrases are for Taro

part one:

when in danger

I

Not having been invited, it's a matter of the utmost importance how I leave.

— Frank Barlow

At the exact moment Jimmy Lafly, Jr. jumped from the Cass Street Bridge, thirty pigeons launched out and up from the beams above in an arc so grand – especially in relation to the plummeting Lafly – that Spleen wound up watching the birds instead of his fellow falling mortal. Spleen took the diver's escape for granted – the water in late November was terminally cold; already ice clung to the banks downriver and more was advancing in great gray translucent triangles – but, he wondered, were the pigeons going to make it?

Would they fly off, say, to the southwest, over the freezing sloughs and swamps, up over the Minnesota bluffs to farmland silos? No. They would trace helixes in the air over the enterprising disturbance in the water below. And what's more, they'd do it with style and organization, over and over again – until the emergency vehicles arrived at Piggy's Restaurant instead of down by the barge where the stiff was. Then the pigeons would settle back on the beams of the bridge that led terrestrials back to their city.

It should be mentioned, in Spleen's defense, that he was at least half a mile by water from his suicidal acquaintance, and three miles by land. He did not know it was Lafly Junior, and he could not have saved him. Had he set out immediately, he would have arrived about the time the last witnesses were being interviewed by Detective Stratton, whose partner, the black undercover cop in the white city, waited in the car. By then Darwin Ness, the Lafly family dentist, would have been shivering in a car on his way home.

"It took two and a half hours under a hot shower for Darwin's balls to drop down," Lafly Senior told Spleen a month later from his position of slouching propriety behind the desk at the rear of Lafly's Antiques.

Several watches arranged on the desk were busy suggesting a kind of mystic and mercenary collaboration of symbolic metals.

"This one here's ten dollars," Lafly said.

"I told you," Spleen told him, "I don't need another watch."

Lafly looked over his shoulder at a clock set into a ceramic chicken and resumed fiddling with the watch.

[3]

"He was too cold to drive himself home," Lafly went on. "Another one of his patients, Rhonda, was there. She had to take him."

"What was she doing there?"

"She saw Jimmy jump same time Darwin did. She drove down there right behind him."

"So your dentist is having an affair with – "

"Darwin's not having an affair. I had dinner with him and his wife last night. Rhonda just happened to be behind him at the time."

"That's quite a coincidence," Spleen said. "They were both crossing the bridge, one behind the other, they both saw Jimmy jump, they both arrived by the barge to look for him . . . but it's all coincidence. She hadn't even been in to see him that day."

"Goddamnit," Lafly began, his mouth stretching laterally to accommodate the force of his exasperation, "how the hell would I know. It's no more coincidence than him being Jimmy's dentist. You think Jimmy waited till someone he knew drove by before he jumped? Alls I know is Darwin was too goddamn cold to drive his own car home."

"He's a brave man. I don't know if I would've jumped in."

"It's a good thing – the minute your balls start to shrivel . . ."

Spleen heard a customer enter behind him and turned. Lafly stood and hitched up his pants. A slim brunette dressed in black moved up the narrow path between shadowy goods with deft officious strokes of all four of her limbs. Spleen thought of both the martial arts and the bland curiosity of fish. It looked as if he'd have to move.

"Everything's on sale today," Lafly drawled.

So, having no idea the leaper was Lafly's boy, Spleen watched pigeons. "That's one way out," he mumbled, then stood, put a cigarette in his mouth, and frisked himself for matches. Lafly Junior was probably halfway to shore by then. His body temperature was probably down to ninety-five degrees. Dentist and patient Rhonda were trying to navigate their ways between the city and the river, bearing with the lassitude presented by an obviously futile situation. It would've been different had it been summer, but a suicide off the bridge in late fall had every chance to succeed. Still, they had to look.

As Spleen was walking away, though, the thought occurred to him: what about the pigeon picked off by that hawk this morning? He turned and looked: the pigeons were still circling in the sky over the bridge. Had he just seen a man jump into the river? He had to think a moment. Had he ever had to bear witness to a death before? By that time Lafly Junior was closer to shore than Spleen would've guessed. Spleen scanned the water down river and saw nothing. Must've gone straight down, he figured. What he couldn't have known was that Lafly Junior was a strong swimmer and that as soon as he hit the water he changed his mind about suicide, squirmed out of his jean jacket, and swam in what his surprised and disoriented brain thought was the quickest way home. Spleen decided to wait and watch for emergency vehicles; with all the traffic somebody must have seen the guy jump, somebody closer to a phone at least. He sat down again, unaware that Lafly Junior's body temperature was already below ninety degrees.

Spleen's hands were cold and chapped. He was enjoying his cigarettes less. He was born on a farm and kept there, for a long time, but his hands were still cold and chapped.

[5]

People like Spleen were deceptive that way. When it's cold out and they aren't wearing gloves you figure they just don't mind the cold, maybe because they were born on a farm or something. Maybe after a while they get numb. Or their hands get like leather. No. In Spleen's case he went into it numb. Cold hands were to him a small matter. He still wasn't over the morning's pigeon assault in the catalpa tree. If these other pigeons had known about it, they'd be long gone by now. But here they were, circling in the sky, winged morons, going nowhere.

He stroked the stubble on his chin. Neither hands nor face registered this.

He hadn't shaved for six weeks and still there was only a little stubble on the chin. He wore a crew cut and kept his face shaved in warm weather. In winter he accommodated the cold, wearing his hair long and growing a full beard. This is a skill many mammals lost in the transition. Now Spleen seemed to have lost it, too. Nothing was growing back. In two days the stubble came out on his chin, but then it stopped. Same on top of his head. He consulted two friends about it. One, Roman, told him to see a chiropractor. The other, Gerard, guessed it was a vitamin deficiency. Spleen sat in the cold, waiting for the sound of tardy sirens, thinking he had a vitamin deficiency.

On top of everything else.

On top of everything else this seemed a small matter. He did not believe in omens, not per se. He didn't look for them. In fact, he probably had only thought about omens two or three times in his life (when Lafly leaped, Spleen was twenty-nine). What he decided was that if something was an omen he'd know; if not before the result, then after. It didn't matter. And it was a wise decision, relieving him somewhat of the burden of apprehending the world.

I'd guess that by now pigeons are involved in most urban omenic displays.

Consider what happened to Roman, since he's already been implicated. His sensitivity to omens was already unparalleled. Here are three examples: when his cat, Ophelia, farted aloud in her sleep, Roman prepared for three days of bad weather ("It can be demonstrated empirically," he would insist – a sign of sufferable lunacy, a connection once made can't be broken, a private gauge of Roman's gloom); when the checkout girl at the grocery handed him back too much change, it meant that those who had cheated him in the past were beginning to make amends; and, perhaps more mundane, when he slept through his alarm something was telling him not to work that day.

Roman was also inordinately sensitive to toxicity. He ate nothing that had had contact with aluminum, ran his faucets at least ten minutes before drinking tap water, and more than anything else lived in dread of pigeon shit, a dollop of which on the tongue, he claimed, could kill a man.

The point is he was driving his taxi one day when a pigeon flew up between his legs after struggling out from under the seat. It was summer and the windows were up because the air-conditioning was on, so the flight of the bird was especially interesting geometrically. It bumped Roman's left calf, angled up and over to his right arm, where it left a lethal streak, then shot straight for the window, which sent it back in a parabola onto Roman's lap. Roman took in the event in a jumbled, nearly lateral time arrangement, something like: a pigeon!, shit on my arm, that's what hit my leg, something hit my leg, it's a fucking pigeon!: and only reacted when he saw the bird on his lap, lying for a moment like something porcelain fallen over on a pillow. His first reaction was to strangle it, and he would have, had the bird not recovered as Roman began pulling over and stumbled up Roman's belly full of blind and warbling menace, falling over backwards before somehow generating what it took to fly madly inside a closed vehicle without knocking itself out. Roman got lucky – when the pigeon startled him this second time he gassed the cab, which jumped the curb and sideswiped a sign that caught between the fender and the body. It could've been a lot worse. The cab didn't stall or hit a tree. His brain didn't snap. The bird was quickly exhausted – it fell panting on the back seat. Roman grabbed it with his right hand and drove back to the cab lot steering with his left, forgoing directionals. He already knew his career was over. Gone were the days when a black pigeon perched on the antenna early in the morn to warn a man his taxi days were finished. Roman drove back to the lot intent on ditching the cab and driving home to work his revenge on the bird in the privacy of his bedroom. Meet your enemy head-on like Charley Varrick. It works if the Joe Don Baker figure isn't omniscient. The pigeon wasn't omniscient. When Roman pulled into the lot the pigeon was, in fact, dead, squeezed until a pencil could not have been inserted in its place. Wet things it had kept inside were on Roman's hand.

Here's where Roman's brain did snap. But only for about five minutes. The dispatcher came out of the office to watch the last two or so, Roman using the uprooted Hwy 6 sign on the little feathered corpse.

Point being that he quit.

(Omen.)

And, because of exits, omens, cab drivers, and birds: once Spleen was in a cab with a driver from the wildcat rival company, Courtesy Cabs (yellow and black). It was after three in the morning, and Spleen had found himself on the North Side, far from any main drag. He'd had some vague notion of dining at an obscure eatery which he wasn't surprised to find closed. But Spleen, as moral moderns do, applied his sense of constancy to an arbitrary moment, walked all the way to a Joie de Gas, picked up a microwave sammy and a cup of coffee, and returned to the steps of the eatery to dine.

But he didn't want to walk home.

A pay phone was nearby.

The cab driver told Spleen the story like a man whose desperation hoped to expire on a long night on a boat in a harbor, at the damp feet of gloomy listeners, in a fog, undozing.

"The beauty of it," he told Spleen, who understood.

The hack's face was moving through an arcade of lights.

"The comedy."

Spleen was happy to have discovered a thoughtful man at such an hour.

"The symmetry. No – the sardonic mocking of symmetry. The up and down. The parabola of death. Or arc. The sound heard against the windshield. The sound not heard – a streak in the rearview mirror – eventually: *eventually,* do you understand – *after* the last possible moment. The splat on the street . . . no, that's mundane, false – *thump* . . . or – *after* the last possible moment – expectations subverted, what went up stayed – my eyes about to return to the street

[9]

before me – then: straight down. A lethal streak. A streak of death, a shabby brown feathered sack of organs recently quit or persevering only from habit, winding down – let's give him kidneys, doing one last time or two whatever it is that kidneys do – but dead. Dead on impact so we don't have him dragging himself with that utmost, that saddest kind of futility, toward the curb, to him an insurmountable escarpment, but if only he could climb it, make it just that far, if only, then – nothing. Too much. Won't do. Leave him dead on the street, dead instantly from the impact – he flying thirty, forty, fifty miles an hour, my cab doing twenty-eight (this was on Seventh Street) directly into him. Dead. Flies up. I see it before me, eclipsed by the roof of the cab, instinctively look to the rearview mirror. How high did he go? Eventually – can you feel it, the delay? Eventually streaking straight down, a bisector of death slicing my rearview mirror."

The driver, hunched over the wheel, steering with the underside of his left forearm, gesturing with his right, driving slowly, ten to fifteen in a 25, to make it last, to expand the night by attenuating the moments with Spleen between their arbitrary beginning and end, so he could continue, "Because it has meaning, *meaning* you under-stand. An event, sickening, beautiful, hilarious in a slap-stick, imagistic way . . ."

Somehow he knew Spleen understood. He looked into Spleen's eyes, therefore, asking for much more, asking him to absorb it, to feel it, to pry more of the weight of its sig-nificance off him, hold it long enough so that he could lurch out from under it, now that it had been lifted and could so easily be set back down awkwardly, painfully, maybe smash something atrophied but amusing.

". . . a moment, an event . . . of power. Force imposed on me from without. It must mean something. And it was delivered, to me – me. You understand – this specificity of impact – it happened to me and I cannot determine its meaning. There is feeling, experience, sufficient unto themselves, and then there is the what-to-make-of-it . . ."

"So you wonder what it was telling you?"

"No. Not that at all. I see what you mean. No, in and of itself, not causally – no. I don't believe in omens. I have my humility."

Spleen, though not himself a cab driver, could be found on the arc/spectrum/continuum of omens somewhere between these two hacks, as partially exhibited in the morning on the day Lafly Junior left the bridge, when he perceived unmistakably an omen in the graceful terrifying flurry of activity in the upper reaches of the catalpa tree outside the bathroom window. In the same way the inversion of the predatory expected is accomplished by the secretary bird which *runs* after its prey, the hawk rushed down from outside Spleen's periphery to murder a pigeon that had somnambuled its way onto an exposed catalpa branch, sending shockwaves through Spleen's notions of territory and pecking orders and a safe world of mundane gambits. The pigeon, quintessential urban bird, struck down by a creature of the marsh, the forest, the prairie, assaulted in the city, in a backyard, right outside a bathroom window. Who should not be affronted?

Spleen wiped himself perfunctorily, pulled up his pants, and ran down the stairs, out the door into the backyard. The hawk was still there, smugly displaying its talents, its death-grip balancing act.

Spleen lurched beyond frontiers of ineffectuality –

"Get the fuck out of here!" Spleen screamed, and looked about for something to throw.

– Nothing was to be achieved there.

While he was collecting wood chips from the neighboring lawn the hawk retreated to a telephone pole in the alley.

"Get the fuck out of there!" Margo Zimmer screamed at Spleen. He'd stolen her wood chips before.

The wood chips sailed like little hawks when Spleen threw them. None came very close to the birds, but after a while the hawk carried the dead pigeon off anyway, this time to a hackberry tree in the front yard of a house across the alley from Spleen's.

"Asshole," Spleen muttered, and gave up whatever it was he was trying to do.

What was he trying to do? Crouch down effeminately into the child he'd forgotten, the child ridiculed into the basement of a farmhouse where he still wept against peas and frigid mornings and arbitrary strictures that always favored others who seemed more stolid, emotionally untouchable, and who never seemed to suffer? Or was he standing his hominid ground, flaunting his spiritmammal freedom to say no and no again to a deliberate and unassailable Yes that ever had its way with him, could swat him about at will, leap out at him from behind nothing, encourage him to believe in little winged niceties, wait patiently to deliver the aren't-you-forgetting-something, but could never, never force him to say yes?

Who knows.

The whole incident just pissed him off and he went for a long walk to be alone (in human terms), off with better birds, beauteous birds, blue birds (but not all that blue, really), public birds with private lives, off away from human terms to blue heron terms, great terms, since anyway he felt he never felt what a human feels, fully, the less so, to the good, when he went off to watch the herons dance low in the sky in their secret slough between the Island and the little islands, over the river where no one but him ever saw them. What others saw were two blue herons. One mantis aslant and still, fastidiously lurking – you can tell by the way their stick legs temporize that the herons would really rather fish and frogs lived elsewhere – the presumption being the bird is hunting, though there's no proof, for no one's ever seen them strike. They know you're watching, and they don't like you. You can tell something about their attitude when you see them in flight, their other pose, rather disdainfully high and straight, the shortest distance over the city, no fancy flight tricks, laugh all you want at their rubber chicken legs. But in private – ah, when alone – the blue herons concocted fluid contortions of balletic splendor below the tree line, gracing their sloughs with an operatic dance, maneuvering in-flight horizontally a contract-and-expand reminiscent somewhat of the head-bob of the mating duck, except the legs were exposed, extended straight out, fluttering rapidly; as well as a group *Tosca* scene, the central heron figure suspending itself looking skyward while a dozen somber nunlike cronies stalked and nodded behind in rough belltoll time – and always, eventually, a breakdown into utter cavorting: running dives off the shore, belly flops, dunking, fish-flinging, fartbubbling, and Spleen-baiting meant to imply that no one would believe him were he ever to open his mouth.

"Where've you been?"

"You wouldn't believe me if I told you."

That's how it worked.

Imagine, then, the emptiness Spleen felt after walking three miles from the morning catalpa massacre onto the Island, across the Island, through acres of woods lining the west side of the Island, only to find that the blue herons had migrated. November and bare trees, ice melting down river and in wait, uncertain sky light gray or unforthright sun (who could tell?), cold farmer hands and empty stomach, an itch born of haste and neglect, cigarette headache, no coffee, collectivity of urban ills, crabs of destitution – no resonant memory torture, yet knowing full well they hold carnivals in places like Brazil, with wide-hipped women who shake tiny breasts wearing silver fezzes over just the nipples, tiny tiny fezzes, and all the men's shirts are unbuttoned, and swilling rum is like monkeys dancing in butter, and no one sings off key, and the parrots are a mélange of pastels that melt in your esophagus, and loneliness, loveblossom, is a very thin, specific syrup dripping from a palm frond right onto your very own tongue. And cold Spleen wondering how a guy gets in on something like that; Spleen wondering how many people hate him; Spleen rolling the phrase "elaborate hoax" around in his mouth, a marble at first, then a pearl that keeps getting bigger, as they do accretionately, bigger and bigger until he can't open his teeth wide enough to get rid of it; Spleen singing "Who's the private dick who's a sex machine to all the chicks?"; a crow overhead, in passing, passing by, answering, "Shaft"; Spleen looking up, then down river half a mile to the Cass Street Bridge, Lafly leaping, and thirty pigeons making the wrong decision.

Man overboard.

With his jean jacket off so he could swim, Lafly Junior headed for a barge next to the granary. Instead of swimming the easy way, straight toward shore so that some kind of vector factor would be established and he'd be taken somewhat downstream, south of the bridge, he swam against the current, heading for the barge that was docked three hundred yards north of the bridge. It was an amazing feat of swimming that in itself nearly killed him. When he first punched his hand against the greenslimed barge his body temperature was probably down near eighty-five degrees. On the other side of the barge his dentist gaped lugubriously, figuring whoever it was who jumped was doomed.

"But then Jimmy started making animal noises and Darwin – "

"Animal noises? What do you mean?"

"That's what he said. A sound like he'd never heard before, like an animal."

"Like an animal what? Howling, groaning, what?"

"He just said like an animal."

"Yes, but was it terror? Anguish? Was he screaming for help?"

Lafly Senior leaned back in his chair. It was already the case that most of his words seemed weary of irony. He resumed patiently.

"He probably finally realized he was going to die. He had no strength left. He was damn near frozen, he could barely move. Darwin had to wait for him to make his way around the barge before he could help him . . . He sent Rhonda to the restaurant to call an ambulance."

"Piggy's."

Even the day of the leap Spleen knew that both possibilities were insupportably funny. The ambulance goes to where the phone call was made rather than the death scene; or a man leaps from a bridge at about the same time another man chokes on his pork; or better yet the man sees the leaper and in the excitement chokes on his pork. Cause and effect. Irony. Ambulance is called from restaurant to save drowning man. Arrives to find choked man dead. Now too late for drowning man. All dead. Throw Darwin into the drink. Fails to save Lafly Junior. Next patient. Back from calling ambulance, leaps in to save dentist. Let the affair begin here. Ambulance rushes to barge, saves woman who called. Dentist saved. Choking man revives, rushes up, Lafly pulled from drink, revived by choking man. No one escapes.

"Christ, you were raised on a farm, you know what it's like for your hands to get so cold you can't hold on to anything. Jimmy's body temperature was down to eighty degrees. He couldn't grab the stick. Darwin had t – "

"Was he still making animal noises?"

What was with Spleen and the animal noises? He imagined something haunting and canine, something canine and lonesome; it tried barking and a horsefly flew into its mouth. Spleen wanted to be happy. He wanted to make that noise. He wasn't happy. He wasn't making that noise.

It's inexplicable.

Even considering his past.

A cock is a big mean chicken worthy of respect. Spleen's old man had his first heart attack while trying to bludgeon a king rooster named Wes. He had a baseball bat in his hands. Wes had pecked him. His hand was bleeding. Spleen's old man didn't know he was having a heart attack – he knew he was too tired to chase a cock around with a baseball bat. Pain from the pecked hand shot up his arm. As country folk will do, he turned to the shotgun. Naturally he was pulling the trigger when the attack laid him down (face first). It hurts pretty bad. He killed one of Wes's paramours instead of Wes. Spleen remembered two things that happened later, after dark. He remembered what it meant to eat that chicken (nothing), and he remembered his father's surprisingly wise words over the phone concerning Wes: "Don't kill him, son, I want no acts of retaliation . . . This war stops now." What's most believable about the episode is the personalized response to the dumb provocations of an animal. For a while, during high school, Spleen was nicknamed "Snapper" by the town kids because it was learned that he, like lots of farm kids, sometimes got mad at cows while milking them and snapped their tails, broke their tails with his cold bare chapped hands. What matters here is that right after the gun went off there was nothing to hear but the fearful scuttling of chicken feet, not a single cluck; and that the cows bore their punishment in silence abject or disdainful or something, but without vocalized agony. Spleen knew not the sound of an agonizing animal. Yet he did know that noise Jimmy was making – he knew that what was really inside him was not crouched but hunched, and it was shuddering its ribs, wanting to make that unhappy noise that issued forth after despair had a chance to get accustomed to the darker side of things.

"There's no way to tell," Lafly Senior continued, "but if Darwin hadn't jumped in Jimmy would be dead."

And Fingers Furlong, the reporter at the scene, who interviewed Darwin Ness while his balls were still burrowing up toward his abdomen, would not have written a story that said: "'He was making sounds like an animal,' Ness said."

And Billy Verité, a bony-faced lad with horse teeth who heard the commotion over the police-band radio and rushed to the scene from the Greyhound station, would not have been able to identify the body with Furlong's help, would not have been able to determine that the attempted suicide was not a fugitive from the law.

"What the fuck are they talking about?" the black undercover cop (in the white city) would not have been asking Detective Stratton when he returned to the car.

"Animal noises."

"So the little snitch is sniffing after suicides now."

"Suicides – say, suicides are confidential. Maybe we should have a word with Mr. Media."

"Wasn't a suicide."

"Huh?"

Maybe Stratton was thinking of something else. Maybe his mind wasn't all there. Maybe he was thinking about a waitress who was a little unstable, who was unable to make certain distinctions, who could, though, understand what she had to fear if she cost him his wife and his job. Maybe. Or maybe he was just stupid.

"The stiff's still alive. That makes it not suicide."

"That don't make it not our business. That don't make it not confidential."

"True. But neither not not our business, nor not not confidential."

"Right. Fuck it. Anyway, he's on our side, isn't he?"

"That don't make him not our business."

"So we bide our time?"

"Right."

"I'll visit him when they let him go to a halfway house," Spleen said.

He turned from Lafly Senior and found no room to exit, for the slim brunette moving with deft officious strokes of all four of her limbs was approaching again between decomposing arrangements of things like antiques.

Her arms and legs became still when she arrived at Spleen, who looked down at her lips.

"I saw the whole thing," she said.

2

I spent last night with the police . . . It was their idea.

— Marlowe, in *Murder, My Sweet*

Remember this, Spleen?

"Twenty-eight years old and you don't have the courage to tell your friends – and that Japanese bitch – to leave so we can be alone. You're so fucking weak. You want to be with me you have to show it, but you cared more about your 'solitary friends' and that woman who even after I told you what she said to me you let her in your house where you knew I was coming and humiliated me in front

of her after what she said to me even though you knew –
shit! I don't even know . . . You're weak!

"Look at me. You're afraid even to look at me. Sure
you look . . . You can't even look me in the eye. A coward,
that's what you are, but that's not the way you see it, no –
you think it's courage. It's so courageous to refuse to work,
such an act of rebellion. You're such a rebel. Well it *is* an
act. The truth is you're weak and afraid, afraid to try to
succeed at anything so you call it an act of rebellion against
an unjust world – well it's the same fucking world *I* live in –
you think *I* like it? You don't think *I'd* like to go without
working half the time? But I'm not a coward, I'm not afraid
of success, I don't have a brother whose happiness and success and kindness frighten me, make me afraid to – shit!
Why do I even fucking . . ."

Boy was she mad. Remember?

"That's what it is, isn't it – your brother, the one with
the talent and brains to leave this dump but who sticks
around because you can't be trusted to look after your father. You're intimidated by your brother. There can only be
one strong one and it's obviously him so you have to be the
weak one so you pretend to reject the whole system, as if
you can claim a different birthright, as if you can be mister
urban survivor, the urban rebel, the ultimate modern man,
this false stance of yours that you do so well and now it's
true, here you are, modern fucking man, and look what he
turns out to be: a 'pathetic wreck,' to use one of the phrases
you like to repeat till you make me want to puke . . .
Modern man: Spleen, a jobless, directionless, dishonest,
posing coward. You're as modern as can be; you're the end,
the last man, the man afraid to create, afraid to exist, who

[21]

rejects everything, even life, but is too hypocritical to commit suicide. But don't think for a minute I expect you to see *that* contradiction, no, then you'd have to choose life or death, you'd have to have *guts* to make that choice, not . . . By the way, where is that Japanese bitch – is she here?"

You pulled a cigarette from the pack, put it between your lips. Then you removed it, held it before you, rolled it back and forth, set it down on the table.

"I hope she is. I really do. She's perfect for you. God, to think I once was, thought I was . . . No, not now, not now that I know you – or don't know you. More like don't. What's there to know? Yeah, she's perfect. Fucking perfect . . . Disloyal prick . . . Some little geisha to wait on you, someone who cares so much for you you don't have to care for me – remember telling me you cared for me? Maybe you did once or twice but you never acted like it. How many times did I cry and you think giving advice was comfort? It's 'cause you don't fucking care. I used to wonder – you worked wonders for my self-esteem . . . The worst kind of man . . . Only later I realized it was you not me, you're incapable of love, incapable of caring – especially if it means you have to change your plans, like the time you thought golfing was more important than seeing me when I was depressed when I needed your love most and then I find out you never went golfing at all, you and Gerard went 'hiking.' Bullshit! You can't even be honest about not wanting me. You never even had the guts to say no I don't want to see you – "

Now you were confused. There were matches in your hand, but the cigarette was gone.

"– tonight I'm doing this instead. It was always, I'd like to see you but I have to read . . . fucking bullshit,

man, you want to read, go to school like your brother did –
you know, the one with a wife, a job, children, a house –
the one who's *happy,* the one who's exactly like you only
happy. But let's not forget happiness is transient, let's not
forget we're all gonna die, let's not forget life is so meaningless all there is is freedom like yours to be a loser, freedom
like yours and Roman's and Gerard's and especially that
fucker Barlow's – all your goddamn friends, all the free and
lonely miserable men you sit around with having miserable
discussions with so you don't have to masturbate all day,
talking about nothing but bullshit that ends up the same
way every time, that life is meaningless so you all end up
prefes– *perpetuating* your own goddamn misery that you
blame on anything but yourself when all it is is . . . is covering up your fear which is so fucking obvious anyway to
anybody but you – "

Where'd you put the matches? Now that you had the
cigarette back between your lips, didn't you have enough
energy to check your shirt pocket? (That's where you put
them.)

"– yet the only good that ever comes out of it – even
that you ruin – you ruin everything you touch; you . . . you
belabor things, to use your favorite word. Every time you
say something interesting you remember it and repeat it
over and over till I want to puke. An example? You want an
example? That's right, *don't* look at me, don't look me in
the face, don't face anything. What a hypocrite. That's what
you hate people for most, isn't it? Not facing things? A hypocrite and a coward, that's what you are. When I quit
smoking you never even thought about it because you did-
n't have the guts to quit, you never thought about what I
was going through. You think it was easy? I just didn't

complain, that's all. You? You wouldn't even try to quit . . .
Christ, I don't even know what I was saying – you and your
friends, repeating yourself, cows in a scrum – you thought
that was so funny, well that's what you and your friends
are, cows in a scrum . . . you must have said that every
fucking day. At least I had the sensitivity to overlook it. But
whenever the slightest thing about me bothered you, no
matter how petty, you had to comment on it until I was
afraid to make a move for fear of appearing too normal,
middle-class, conventional, conformist – you called me
everything at one time or another. Well, fuck you! I'm
through with that. I'll be whatever you want me to be except pathetic like you – or pathetic with you – "

What if you were a dog? How long would a dog sit
there stupefied before such excoriation? Would a dog turn
and walk away? Or would he put his head on his paws and
look up at her with his brown eyes?

"– like you wanted me to be, like you were so dishonest
about trying to make me be, like you . . . you lied about it,
you lied about everything. You abused me. Every time you
fucked me it was abuse. It was worse than rape. It *was*
rape. You misrepresented yourself: it was never you I made
love to. I'd never open myself to someone like you. Now
that I know you, you couldn't even make me wet. Every
time I see you now the very thought of sex makes me sick. I
don't want to fuck anybody anymore because I think of
you and it makes me sick. It couldn't be worse if I was
raped on the street – oh God, you raped me! You're a fucking rapist! Look at me! You raped me! And you don't
fucking care . . . well neither do I. You think I care, but I
just want to tell you one last time: you're a piece of shit.
You can sit there and not feel a fucking thing. Because

you're so strong? So detached? No – because you're nothing. You aren't even there. There's nothing to you. You have no self. You've been a goddamn fake for so long you don't even have yourself. You know where it is? It's your brother, that's where your self went. Off to be a good man, someone people can look up to and trust and care about, someone who cares about others and can handle life with strength and courage and and – I don't know what, anything but the fucking cipher you are . . ."

You looked up, not quite at her face, but up that way. You'd never heard her say the word "cipher" before.

"– which is the whole thing right there: you're nothing, a phony – whatever I see, whatever anyone sees, always and for the rest of your miserable life, is a lie, a fake, a pretense. You shave your beard and cut your hair and then you grow it all back, grow your hair long – why? Because you don't know who the fuck you are. You're empty, nothing – a fucking cipher. That's why you have nothing to say right now. All you can do is react, but you can't react to the truth, can you? Go ahead, react. Say something. You can't do it, can you? There's nothing there. Nothing at all. Well, I don't have anything to say either. I'm not going to fill your life up anymore. I'd end up just like you. You drain me. You make me feel like nothing, like you, like I'm not with a man at all – I'm more alone than ever. How many times do I walk in here and you can't even greet me, just stare at me like you're stupid, like you don't even see me? What the fuck was I doing here? You can't even make me feel wanted. I never felt wanted, not after the first two months when you were acting – *acting* – like a real human being, which was all a goddamn lie, like you told me you were through with that bitch and when it comes down to it you choose her over me because you say she needs you and now I do – Christ! I don't even know what I'm . . ."

And just like that she left and it was forever over. But another woman was bound to come along.

The way what passes for meaning is arrived at: Spleen reading on the toilet, absently fondling himself, coming across a question in the book he's reading – "Why, we must ask ourselves, have individuals of unquestionably great powers chosen to play with their minds like captive monkeys with their genitalia?" – so taken by the coincidence that he copies the quote and tapes it to the water heater that dominates the small bathroom with the slant ceiling, that phallically lodged like a lidless silo looms a brilliant white before the stool of the defecator, this time the Sneering Brunette, whose hands rested between her thighs as she bent forward above her own inflamed genitalia.

It was that certain sneer to her lips that made them less thin, which was what it was that attracted Spleen long enough to look long enough at her that he lost track of his distractions and caused him to listen when she told him she had been parked at Riverside Park when the attempted suicide took place.

"I didn't know it was your son," she told Lafly Senior over Spleen's shoulder.

Spleen tried to dance his torso well out of her line of sight, there being too little room in the aisle to shift enough to let her pass without premature contact. But her head with its sneering lips seemed to deliberately thwart his maneuvers. It turned out she was preparing to deliver her next line to him. If he would only hold still.

"I was watching you, too. I could see your figure in the rearview mirror. Of course, I didn't know it was you."

Geographically, she was a lone point of woman between two lone points of man.

"Where were you?" Spleen finally asked.

"I was parked at Riverside Park," she said.

A long pause ensued during which Lafly made an involuntary sound much like the jowly fluttering coon hounds make before they flop down befuddled on a hard bed not too far from the fire. Without explanation he slipped away. Spleen and the Sneering Brunette heard his feet descending stairs.

Spleen looked down at the Sneering Brunette. He was willing to wait a long time to see what was next.

"I've moved a lot since then," she said eventually.

"I've moved once," Spleen said, establishing between them the special ability to drift together without regard for the impingement of lucid misgivings. Even as he said it he marvelled at the dumb intransigence of the space between what is known and what would be helpful if known. It was an odd thing for her to say and he let it be his guide all the way from Lafly's antique store to his bed, where she was on her stomach and he was on her back and his mute mammalian lungings were bringing his head closer and closer to the wall until he had to ask her to slide down, which she did serpentine and raising her nates up so that his lunges were executed more deep and perilous, though he only knew for sure how perilous when she yelped, "My spleen!" – an exact reference to something inside her, he knew, because he had not told her his name, though knew only after a moment not unlike the trickery of déjà vu, and knew, as a consequence, as one of the stranger moments he'd ever experienced naked.

The oddness lasted – it was like swatting at a single timid mosquito in the dark. While the Sneering Brunette was on the toilet reading the quote on the water heater over and over until quite by accident she'd made sense of it, Spleen was on the couch in the next room beset by a series of mental shudders.

He needed to make contact with someone from the outside.

"Try the shower," he called out, "not because you stink, but you wouldn't believe the pressure. It's like a fire hose."

The first time Spleen had used it, two days after Lafly Junior had taken his dive, one day after he'd finally left Roman and the Red House, the malicious and aptly focussed jet of warm water had caught him off guard and sent him reeling. Life, Spleen thought, his very persistence at it, his simple refusal to leap, was a stubborn protest against some shiftless authoritarian who was now hosing him down like he was someone caught watching a riot.

He was unclean and he knew it.

"I don't need a shower," the Sneering Brunette said, coming through the doorway a different kind of unclean. "I like to keep the smell on me. I like the way it feels."

Spleen, blank and unexpectant – healed – could not have suggested anything he would rather have heard.

Her hair fell over her shoulders, stopping where her breasts, thirty-five years old each, sloped downwards and out to nipples hard from the endurance of rapid climatic change. Before Spleen had over-prodded her sensitive innards, she had been on top of him, her hair circumscribing his face in the candlelight; and though he recognized the transmutation of gratitude into something false and sublime – which always happened to him when he had sex again after a time long enough that he found himself bowed pathetic before a death that refused to come – the way she looked at him through the strands of hair, as if she were not afraid to face her pleasure even if it meant the breaking of fine things and a series of beatings, as if there were something to be had that was tougher and less trite than ecstasy, made Spleen imagine spotting that hair from a distance bobbing across the street on a head still daffy from its landing, and spotting it again on a different head, spotting it again and again everywhere he went, the great dark bird of his daylight torment that would swoop and leap from head to head until – as he saw it from inside her hair, pinned down in a rodent's resignation by her eyes – he would awaken from a liquor dream in a trapezoid of green light on a motel room bed long soiled and crusty with the untidy scutellation of her departure.

And now this: the same woman, a woman who didn't have to hose herself down immediately after. Spleen knew he liked her, and he was not afraid. She was a woman who kept the end in sight.

"My name's Spleen," he said. "No use making too much of it."

She sat next to him on the couch and kissed him the way a sloppy alcoholic does just before passing out.

"That'll do for now," she said, after releasing his lips.

Spleen looked along the crease of her belly.

"You have a girlfriend, Spleen?"

"No."

"You want one?"

"Maybe for a while."

She tilted her head back and laughed both demure and equine. Spleen had never before witnessed such a laugh. There was longing in it, and reluctant grace.

"Perfect," she said. "I'm thirty-five."

"Boyfriend?"

"Not for a month. He threw me out the night before the suicide."

Spleen looked down at her hand, resting on his bare thigh, an inch or two from his penis, which was flopped that way. The two, penis and hand, looked like extras for a still life, like together they'd been neglected before.

"You're the kind of woman who finds it easy to assume intimacy," he told her.

"You've been off the farm a long time, haven't you?" she replied.

"What gave it away?"

"Your hair. And the way you walk – like you're stomping through pigshit."

Spleen looked at a wall.

"Don't get me wrong – I like farmers. I like animals. I've heard all kinds of stories. Ever fuck a sheep?"

"What's the right answer – in your case?"

"I'm serious. I've been told all farm kids have sex with animals. City boys masturbate, farm boys play with their animals."

"Maybe it used to be that way. We got farm girls now. We call them cousins."

Spleen could not gauge her contentiousness.

(She didn't laugh.)

"No, but really – you never even squeezed a sow's tit or anything? Or wanted to?"

"Not that I recall. Is there something you want to get off your chest?"

"I've never *done* it; I just think about it. I wonder what you'd really feel like. If you'd have to be drunk to go through with it. I mean, if it would feel strange, or self-conscious, once you were actually doing it . . ."

Spleen looked down at the hand and penis. Neither had moved. He acknowledged in himself with pleasure the ability to appreciate sincere thoughtfulness wherever he found it.

"What's your . . . what kind of animal . . ."

"Oh, a horse of course. Didn't I say that? I think every woman fantasizes about fucking a horse, it only makes sense."

"Maybe riding one and getting your first orgasm; I don't know about actually fucking one."

"No – fucking. I mean fucking. You know, the whole idea of power and size . . ."

"You know what my dad used to say instead of bullshit? Horsecock, he'd say."

"I don't think it's all that strange. You're not guilty for thinking about it. We think all kinds of things. Although I made the mistake of telling my ex about it, and the crazy bastard actually got jealous. Whenever we passed by horses on the road he'd be watching out of the corner of his eye, just the same as if it was some guy with his shirt off. See if I was sneaking a look. He acted like I was sick. He brought it up whenever we had a fight. Sick horsefucking cunt, he'd call me. He's the one – hey, what's that?"

"What?"

"Open a window."

"It's pretty cold."

"Just for a second."

Before the couch stood a small oval formica table, which Spleen leaned across to open the window.

"No, it's coming from over there.'

Spleen, with the dull half-disbelief of a sleepy child, followed her finger into the bedroom, where he reached the window by bounding the length of his bed on his knees.

"It's like a cabin in here. It's nice . . ."

"You mean that cough?"

"I've never heard one like it. If that's lung cancer I quit smoking tonight – after I get home."

"She does it all night sometimes."

The cough occurred a block away, where it tumbled heavily from a second-story window to cut an inconsolable tubercular swath through the neighborhood. Spleen and the Sneering Brunette had no trouble understanding what was happening. Air best applied to breathing was being used to suck retrograde phlegm off cilia and, against the more vigorous pretenses of gravity, force it upwards. Something wasn't working. It sounded as if discs of mucous rose like alien hovercraft, gained the larynx, and were abruptly destroyed, the pieces reforming in descent into new, disguised shapes, in time for the matter to seek ever deeper pulmonary recesses, wherein they would cling again, and where the laborious and exhausted breaths would eventually find them in order to resume the process.

"Had enough?" Spleen asked, shutting the window.

Now that they were on the bed again, the Sneering Brunette said, "How about once more and you walk me home?"

And when they'd had enough, Spleen said, "All right."

"Can I wear your socks?" she asked.

"Clean ones?"

"No."

"Check my pants."

Spleen, watching where her hips fanned into splayed thighs when she bent over, liked that her body had only two colors, neither of which, he guessed, derived its scumbling from the light of morning. And he knew he would be lying on the bed again someday, just as he was now, head propped against the panelling, wishing the cigarettes were within his reach, and she'd walk through the door, through the rectangle of light tripping out of the bathroom, and before she passed the oval formica table, just as a blanket of damp fur swept through the breach in his thoughts and the carpet tilted forty-five degrees starboard, he would tell her to bring him his cigarettes.

"Get me a cigarette," he said.

And silently they smoked, she straddling him sexlessly, both ashing on the windowsill without taking their eyes off their eyes, both expressionless insofar as possible, neither in wonder, though Spleen was musing abstractedly: over the steppes they came, tribes going up to the mountains to wait for centuries or crossing the mountains to sack the cities of the plains, whence came the Huns who returned to drive off the tribes who filed goat-ridden through Khyber Passes, across Caucasuses and Volgas, Berings and Dardanelles', arriving, never arriving, slipping by Mashhads at night, reconnoitering under ambivalent moons; Spleen then spliced into retreat, a steel skullcap dislodged, when she lifted off and left him helmeted, cervically capped, pointing up to the map of the stars, when he scanned the length of his recumbence, his knees being up, and said look, a little Visigoth, and she laughed and laughed, and that was the last time she did as far as he knew because she sure wasn't laughing last time he saw her, was she?

"What are you smiling at?" the Sneering Brunette asked.

"How we got here."

Spleen certain that the mad proliferation of accident called design renders all experience absurd of course, but bearable therefore; nonetheless utterly astonished that the millennia of slow hominidian disarray had collapsed into this small bedroom in what he was not afraid to call the best apartment he ever lived in.

"Were you thinking of a woman?"

"For a moment or two."

"When was the last time you fucked her?"

"Which her?"

"The one you were thinking of."

"A year . . . longer than that, I think."

"Did you part on good terms?"

"Probably . . . There was a lot I didn't say. There was a lot she did say. She didn't like my friends."

"Were you with her a long time?"

"Yes."

"Do you miss her?"

"No."

"Never?"

"I'm fairly . . . susceptible to fact."

Spleen saw her hair falling toward his face and heard a husk of sound within. Someone's stomach roiled. He hadn't slept recently enough to know if she had asked if he could do it again before her hands were squeezing the flesh around his nipples and her hips were spiralling downward.

Outside the cough was emptying itself of the long night.

"I'm hungry," she said later. "Can I keep these socks?"

"There's that taco place open behind the Dance Building."

"Can I have these socks?"

"Why don't you keep those socks. I've got more."

Despite a sun bulging through the fine falsity of wintry morn clouding, Spleen's socks probably weren't warm enough for either of them, even inside shoes. It was so cold that physical laws concerning melt and shine, passed down subversively through progressively more dupeful generations, no longer applied. Every few steps either Spleen or the Sneering Brunette slipped on lustrous gray carapaces that should not have basked on the sidewalk with impunity.

As they passed a narrow white two-story house that leaned forward on its foundation, Spleen pointed to one of its windows. A lampshade tilted into the glass still gave off a weak spume of light. "I think the cougher lives up there," he said.

And then, so abruptly it seemed simultaneous with the resultant puzzled look on his own face, that very genuine puzzlement that so often makes hard women nearly cry, a white bird fluttered from its perch somewhere down back of Spleen's jaws, an albino pigeon, feathered projectile light as a tongue, flew forth in admission unrequitable: "My father was retarded."

"What?" the Sneering Brunette asked, but Spleen was busy trying to recapitulate the sequence, so obviously unencumbered by reason, that had led him to volunteer such private information to a woman who was even more of a stranger than most.

Spleen was baffled.

"Did you say your father was retarded?" she prompted.

"Did I? I think I did."

The yards they passed were covered by crusted snow, glazed over, and innumerable footprints that spoke for the vanished. There were no people in sight, no cars moving in the streets.

"You did."

"I don't tell people that. I've never told that to a woman."

Doubtless the Sneering Brunette was uncertain what sort of flattery she'd been offered.

"Did you want to talk about it?"

"God no. Not in the least."

In the meantime they had crossed Fourth Street at the corner of Division, where the Dance Building, four stories high and not crumbling, a solid brick building with relatively cheap one bedroom apartments ($295 a month) on the third and fourth floors, stood as a rare testament to the capacity of River City Man to build a simple building downtown neither architecturally ludicrous nor indelicately renovated into something without walls – like a parking ramp – or with more than one hair salon. It was a fine old brick building, commanding from its upper west apartments a view of the river, and in particular, from apartment 414, a view of the Cass Street Bridge.

Attached to the back of the building, on the river side, was a drive-up taco shed, open twenty-four hours.

As Spleen received their parcel of tacos, the Sneering Brunette's face riffled, leaving a wake of concern.

"Where do we eat it?"

"There's a warm car parked over at the Greyhound."

"Really."

"A guy I know, Billy Verité – he'll be waiting on the 7:30 bus. One of the tacos is his. See the exhaust through there? It's from a car that used to be mine."

A blue metal capsule sent puffs of welcome to the sky from behind bare trees lining the Greyhound parking lot on the other end of the block. It was only a matter of getting there.

If such a thing as an Arctic Air Time/Temperature Conversion Table existed, it would be possible to determine that while for Billy Verité, who missed little of small significance within his most blatant periphery, it took them about a minute to reach his car from the taco shed, for Spleen it took two minutes, and for the Sneering Brunette it took almost three.

"Billy," Spleen said as he climbed into his old car, "let us eat here for a taco."

"Hello, Billy," the Sneering Brunette said as she squeezed in after.

Billy had a face so narrow that the Sneering Brunette was compelled to stare at him until she understood how each of her eyes looking straight on could glance past his head and still see him. It's like looking at a playing card from the side, she thought.

Meanwhile, Spleen's first thought as he handed Billy a taco was the same as always when he saw him again: that is the ugliest man I know. The problem was that a head extraordinarily narrow still had to bulge to accommodate a skull that compensated forward and a mouth that slyly mocked sensible notions of normalcy by being in essence typical yet because of things like relativity appearing anything but. Billy's mouth could prompt the most inanely wayward of elderly women to stop dead on the sidewalk and mumble in abject wonder: mammals eat that way. The skin that had to come too far from the cavity starting beneath the brow gave the impression of decadent excess that anything overly stretched would, somehow making the teeth seem unnaturally long and supernumerary (horse teeth). To make matters worse, Billy always wore jeans so tight that most of his genitalia were forced to choose one side; he never wore a coat long enough to cover the bulge, which was stared at involuntarily by good people the way a barely prepustulant tumor would be. Whether Billy was aware of this immodest genital hypnosis is an entirely separate question from that concerning his ability to interpret the phenomenon. What's known is that there was a correlation between the unnatural way Billy wore his pants and the way the skin hung on his face. And yet it can't be overlooked that Billy's unabashedly skinny torso provided a sort of conduit between nodes of disgust that would have been less than spectacular otherwise; or, to put it differently, more mathematical as two repulsives and hence less horrific than, say, the Parasite Lady who chainsmoked at McDonald's wearing a maternity blouse that didn't always cover up the little ass that fell perpetually from about her sternum.

"Hi, Spleen. Thanks. Who's the brunette?"

"Here to crack a big one?" Spleen asked.

"Richard Gerard Bocklage. Alias Dick Bock, Rick Bock, Dick Bocklage, Richard G. Bocklage, Dick Bocklege – aka Richard G. Bocklege, aka Robert G. Cass – Interstate Flight, Capital Murder."

"Let me see the book."

"Page twelve," Billy Verité said, handing Spleen a book called *The FBI's Most Wanted*. It was four inches by two and a half, its cover littered with tiny mugshots of twenty-five of the most dangerous men on the lam in America. Amazingly, the book cost only ninety-nine cents and was available at most supermarkets. It had this to say about our friend Dick Bocklage: "Bocklage is reportedly an avid outdoorsman who could survive in the wilderness for long periods of time. He is being sought in connection with the murder of a female victim who was shot three times in the face with a .45 caliber pistol. Consider him armed and dangerous. Because Bocklage is a survivalist who can live off the land by solitary hunting and foraging, it's always possible that he could still be hiding out somewhere in the wide open spaces as a hermit or recluse. But he's still a young man, and he won't be able to resist the lure of the bright lights forever. So you might spot him some evening as he enters a seedy small-town bar, clad in lumberjack shirt and hiking boots. If that happens, don't get too close. Call the FBI."

"He's got scars under his arms," Billy said, pointing to the top of page thirteen, "but we won't be able to see those. What we have to look for is the nose. See that? Same in both pictures. You don't see many noses like that. He can change his facial hair, but he can't change his nose. He might have a Fu Manchu, or even a Van Dyke, maybe even spectacles . . ."

"Muttonchops?"

"Sure. Sometimes they do that. But the only way we'll be in trouble is if he's wearing a ski mask. If he is, we follow him till he takes it off."

"We?"

"You don't want to come with me?"

"Probably not."

"All right, but if I gotta roll you might not have time to evacuate."

"Billy, what makes you think this particular man will be on the bus?" Spleen asked, turning then to explain how things were to the Sneering Brunette: "Billy's here every day looking for fugitives because in large part that's how a man on the lam travels, by bus, and it's only natural to assume that now and again they'd come through here."

"What if they stay on the bus?"

"Tell her, Billy."

"If I don't recognize someone coming off the bus I tell the driver I'm looking for my little sister who I'm supposed to pick up – the drivers all know me, see – and I make a quick sweep down the aisle."

"And he – "

"Don't you think they'd wonder about you expecting your sister every day?"

"Sometimes I say it's my cousin."

"Oh."

"The main thing is Billy stands to make a lot of money if he finds one of these fugitives. How much is this one worth?"

"Victim's family: 20,000. FBI: 8,000. Crimestoppers: 5,000. That's 34,000."

"You could live off that for five years."

"Two years. Half or more will go to a special security van I'll operate out of in the future, complete with several thousand dollars of surveillance equipment."

"So what makes you think Mr. Bocklage will be the one? Why not . . . Terence Strickland? Says here he's from Chicago – El Rukn."

"I'm partners with a guy in Milwaukee, see. He called me last week. Word on the street is that our local chapter of B.A.D. sent for a hit man. My informant heard this: 'Richie Buck, from Out West.' Richie Buck, from Out West. It's him, I can smell it."

It would not have been surprising in the least if Spleen had not noticed the sudden subtle stiffening of the Sneering Brunette's leg upon mention of the organization B.A.D. Nor would it have been an egregious blunder for him to assume that she was simply in vague fear of the biker menace the same as the rest of polite society. Yet the wise and perceptive move, which he made, was to store the information in a safe place where it would have the opportunity to accumulate into something raw and unavoidable that he could later flee from.

Cops are like that, too, always storing away facts and using them later.

Case in point: when the white undercover cop, Stratton, who with the black undercover cop was staking out Billy Verité and thus bore witness to the impromptu front seat taco indaba from his unmarked gray sedan parked across Cameron Street in the Ford lot, saw Spleen, he thought to himself: now where have I seen that face before?

"Something's going down, pard," he said, to justify his reflections.

"What did I tell you about calling me pard?"

"That you didn't like being called pard."

"Right. And when did we start saying going down?"

"Okay, forget it. Forget it – I won't even tell you how the chief suspect in the biggest unsolved murder case ever in the history of La Crosse just took a seat in Billy Verité's car. I guess that would be a matter of no significance to you. I guess it wouldn't mean a thing to you to take part in solving the greatest – "

"Shut," the black undercover cop said, "up."

"Look, I'm talking about the Sherri Holloway case."

"I know that."

"The one and only suspect ever picked up for questioning, the one suspect with no verifiable, substantiated, or corroborated alibi, is in that car – now you tell me that's a coincidence."

"You will not tell me what to tell you. You will not call me pard. And you will not say going down unless you see something actually falling which if you keep getting on my nerves you might in one moment, and it will be you."

"Jesus, have some more coffee," Stratton said petulantly, falling into a sulk engineered by the mantra, 'I'll just have to make the collar by myself.' And it was a prospect not unlikely if a collar were to be made, since the five-year-old Holloway file was wide open and no one was working on it. Leads still came in, but nine out of ten were from wives and girlfriends associating the drunken strangular gestures of their men with the decapitation of Miss Holloway. Invariably, a detective would patiently explain into the phone that "at one time or another just about every man in this county puts his hands around a woman's throat – that don't make them all homicidal maniacs. Now if you'd like to prefer a charge of simple domestic assault, we can have a deputy out there in no time at all . . . ," by which time the caller would be fully prepared to hang up, for by now a simple domestic assault charge would only further ingratiate her to the big lug. So if Stratton were to act, he'd have to act alone – which, by god, he was used to, having, on his own initiative, searched Spleen's apartment illegally while Spleen was downtown answering questions regarding his whereabouts the night before, that is to say, the night Sherri Holloway disappeared from Piggy's Restaurant, where, perhaps not so coincidentally, Spleen's girlfriend at the time tended bar.

We can call Spleen innocent, and indeed we must, but how could he possibly explain what he was doing all night the night Holloway was murdered? Could he have told his interrogators that he had suddenly encountered in himself a stretch of barren and incomprehensible terrain? That quite abruptly, without warning, and somehow instigated by the discovery of a dead bird in his own rented back yard, his universes exterior and interior flipped and overlapped and he was beset by insights too numerable to decipher intelligibly?

It was the grayest of pigeons and it had no head, though blood recently trickled into the snow formed an ovalish shape that could hydrocephalically have served as one. Spleen, hardly subject to easy illusions, knew right off that the bird had been decapitated; yet what time he could have spent mulling over the possibilities, time spent deducing specifics, was soon eliminated by a powerful wash of generalities when he brought the pigeon into the apartment, put it in the freezer and turned around in time to see his girlfriend, dressed up like a Swiss maid for work, whose head well-established on her neck he suddenly knew harbored vastly ludicrous possibilities of estrangement behind a look composed of familiar vapidities, the effrontery of distraction, and a painted mouth that Spleen realized was telling him not to forget to feed a cat that as far as he knew was not an animal that lived with the two of them.

Responding to his interrogators, then, Spleen condensed several hours of murky and discomfiting motivation into the official statement: "I went driving all night so I could think things over, think about my relationship." He never really thought about the pigeon, but it was there throughout the drive, swooping phantomly, a projectile of withheld and disturbing knowledge, preventing Spleen from concentrating effectively on his unease, in fact perpetuating it like the hirsute insect dispatched by delirium tremens.

He drove as south as the highways would allow, unhindered by the Illinois border, inevitably speeding, eventually sputtering into the mania for repetition that keeps anxiety from breaking down. He played the same tape over and over until about seven hours into the drive he fastened on one song that was arranged like the high-strung laborings of his Volare's engine, a song that asked him:

> Why is it so hard?
> Why is it so hard?
> To love somebody,
> Really love somebody?

and then said:

> It's so easy
> It's so easy
> To do the goat dance

> But it's so hard to love somebody,
> Really love somebody

and kept listening to it, over and over, until he arrived at the slack light of dawn, where he was able to count the empty Old Style bottles, one for each convincing reason drained of significance, one for each afterpuddle of stale conviction: reasons to press on southward, reasons to turn back, the conviction to do anything but lean his face into the clarified reflection of a rearview mirror that asked quite plainly why he had become so thoroughly pathetic. So he drumbled his Volare into the first diner he sensed was devoid of compensations for loneliness, ate hash browns, bacon, eggs, and toast, drank coffee, smoked three cigarettes, got back into the Volare he would eventually sell to Billy Verité for twenty-five dollars more than it was worth, and headed back north, where it was dark enough when he arrived that the detectives were virtually upon him before he noticed them.

His disappearance had alarmed his girlfriend, who had received calls throughout the night about her missing workmate, Sherri Holloway. When Holloway's headless body was found at dusk, smoldering next to the same highway Spleen had taken out of town, detectives quickly made the connection between her gruesome murder and the missing person's report filed by Spleen's girlfriend. Welcome back, Spleen thought, as the handcuffs pinched shut. And as they led him to their car he looked back over his shoulder at the man in the polyester suit with the long blondish hair and misbegotten mustache who was leaning into the dome-lighted Volare, and was now, five years later and clean-shaven, hair short and neat, dressed for the out-of-doors in jeans and a lumberjack jacket, happily drawing out the black undercover cop, successfully altering his churlish mood by trading sex stories about the woman who had left him, Stratton, for this very same partner two years before, but lately had been telling him lies of the kind cops easily expose by abusing their resources.

"She liked it, huh?" the black undercover cop asked through his constricting throat.

"That's not all she liked."

"What else?"

"Well . . . listen to this. You know how crazy she could get. This one time I had her out to the Dakota Motel for the weekend. And we had all these brats left over from the day before when we cooked out at Riverside. I don't know why, we brought them to the motel. Anyway she was pissed at me about something – I guess I left her alone all night or whatever. I was standing by the door and all these brats were in a bowl by the bed, and she's sitting up, crying and screaming, a real fucking mess, and she starts throwing these brats at me – I don't know, I wasn't demonstrating enough remorse or something – she's throwing these brats at me one by one, and I've about had it, so I say cut it the fuck out or I'll shove one of them right up your fucking ass. So she throws one more, just to see if I'll really do it, you know, and so I figure, fuck, I warned her, and I grabbed a brat and turned her over my knee and shoved it right up her ass, all the fucking way; and see at first she's screaming to beat anything, but soon, I mean real soon, she's moving her ass – she realizes she likes it, so I start enjoying it, too, and next thing you know it's all over and we're fucking like goddamn newlyweds . . ."

"She liked it, huh?"

"Hell, yes, she liked it. I'd have stopped otherwise."

"She likes brats, huh?"

"Well, you know, that was the only time . . ."

"Here's the bus."

3

I have picked my feet in Poughkeepsie . . .

— Me

Why pretend. This is my town. I've been back a long time.
Or never left. (I got old fast.) I always end up thinking this
place isn't worth a shit and I always end up back. It's an old
formula: no place is worthy of me; I'm worthy of no place.
It's not a big deal, and certainly not a matter of accepting
this place as my home. To go back and forth, to pretend
otherwise – to allow these spaces, lapses of concentration
and place – is just fine. The urban nomad. To call him that
is to say his home is an arbitrary. Home as where you're

beaten back to, where you foray less and less from. When you're a kid you walk the railroad tracks out of town and the first time you round a bend and lose sight of your city you hear a helicopter overhead and realize you're a fugitive, want nothing more than to be a fugitive. You flatten yourself against a rock until the chopper passes, hoping they didn't see you. Now look ahead: just the other side of that tunnel is freedom. You'll have to move fast; they'll be making another sweep any minute now. All you have to do is cross that railroad bridge. Beneath the bridge is five hundred feet of air and three feet of icy water. Other side: Mexico. Lonely are the brave. Child's play. You're an adult now, and you know it's hard enough as a fugitive in the bosom of Mother City; it only gets harder as you go farther out. You can take the man out of the city, but only the city will accommodate his false notions of civility.

I tried once to get Spleen to walk the tracks with me, just to see him outside the city, see it for myself. But he wouldn't go. The tracks always lead right back in. No matter how far into wilderness you think the tracks have cut, around the next bend or the one after you'll see a familiar chemical tank, or the remains of a warehouse that has seen its best days twenty-nine years before. You're back. You'd think it was uncanny. Not long ago a friend of mine wrote a story about a man for whom a city replicated parts of itself. The man, riding a bicycle and sucking on a trumpet (sucking, to get at its spirit), would see a particular urban configuration at the corner of, say, Union and Grant, and there it would be again, the same facades, the same four corners, at Market and Seventh. Of course, his story meant to dramatize paranoia; but I have seen these replications and I do not fear them. I walk the tracks in other towns and see the same escarpments, tunnels, bridges; and whenever the tracks pass a cemetery I see the same names engraved on the same stones. But I say if you would breathe life into the city to provide organization for your paranoia, why not consider the possibility that the city is more benign than that, perhaps even discouraged; and its replications are a last fey attempt to mean something. The city has its feet planted solidly on ground that, in the case of our city, La Crosse, not even the great glaciers covered; it must know very well its age and fear the decadence it ushered in with it, harboring it the same way we do our own little seed of inglorious death. Is it not possible that each replication can be translated as the cry of the city, "Let me mean something!"? *We* built the cities.

Years ago I visited our courtroom to see what kind of people went there. I saw a man in a blue jumpsuit, jail-issue, a big man with an unreplicable nose, long wild hair, thick frontiersman's beard, standing before the judge. If I had to call him something I would probably say "trapper." The prosecutor called him "pedestrian on the interstate." The big man nodded. It was true. The judge considered that a moment, then asked him where he came from. "Out West," he said. The judge asked what he was doing here, why he had "come East." Without hesitating, the man said, "I came to see the Driftless Zone." And the judge sentenced him to the night he'd already spent in jail.

I told this to a friend of mine, a demographer, who was visiting from Chicago. I wanted to make too much of the Driftless Zone, I suppose; I wanted the refusal of the glaciers to visit our region to have a meaning that resisted the ravages of time and civilization and I thought I spotted that meaning in the high incidence of odd behavior in La

Crosse, a common denominator of what I saw as rugged schizophrenia, which perhaps I glorified as the last vestiges of the primal human spirit perversified by its struggle to break free of the confines of its own deadening strictures. I would've put it better back then, before the onset of these convolutions. Still, no matter how well I put it I was talking to a demographer. He told me that I was witnessing the result of a process common to all small cities. This is pretty much what he said: "A city is defined as much by who has left as by who remains. What you see in small cities – rather, what you don't see – are the beautiful and the talented, those whose virtues are better rewarded elsewhere. For instance, let's say you are an ambitious and capable young man – you're going to want to go to a big city where you can make some money. Let's say you're beautiful – then you go to Hollywood, or latch on to someone with talent, someone who will take you to a big city. If you understand this, you'll see why your leading citizens here always seem grotesque. Those who rise to the top are filling vacancies left by those more fit for those roles. It even extends to your bar queens – your vamps or vixens, if you will. Even your few prostitutes. If you take the average prostitute from Chicago and walk her down the street here, I'll bet nine out of ten people would think she was an actress. I'm sure you can see how broad the implications are – they extend even to the arts: where do you go if you make beautiful music? Where are the symphonies? New York, Chicago, Philadelphia. What all this comes down to is nothing more or less than my specialty – proportion. In proportion, the small city lacks talent, beauty, smarts, the can-do spirit, lovely music . . . What you do have is a high percentage of misfits, fools, various mediocrities, ineptitude, a shabby sort of grandiosity, an enlarged capacity for botching ill-conceived projects. In proportion you'll have more of everything you don't clearly lack, more flashers, peeping toms, dim-witted substitute teachers, petty thieves (the pettiest thieves), vandals – I could go on and on. And from the other end you have the farmers, the replacements. These are the only ones who still have values, only their values no longer apply. As long as they're able to remain on their farms they're all right. But they come here uprooted; their traditions no longer make any sense. They're lost. And as long as people are stuck here, or stick themselves here, farmers or otherwise, they lack vision. They live entirely within this little city and don't see outside it. On the surface there would seem to be equilibrium, but that's not the case. People are too big for the small city – they're overflowing with humanity, with human yearnings, human desires. They don't see out, though, so they compensate inwards and a sort of implosion occurs, which in this case equals perversion. Whenever a life is in this way misapplied, directed entirely the wrong way, it becomes perverse; all the grandiosity of human society is played out on too small a stage. It's like raising an alligator in a terrarium. See any polar bear at the zoo, the way it paces or slumbers larger than life – that's what's happening to the human characteristics in this town; big wild emotions are pacing restlessly in too small environs; or they're sleeping, ostentatiously, or ominously, or pathetically. If you shrink your world to an area of, say, twenty square blocks, you're going to be grievously wrong about everything. Because the world is, simply, the world – Earth, which is floating in space. You forget that, you shrink it down to a size you mistakenly think you can manage, and your vision becomes grotesque. Imagine the map in the mind of the man of your city. Very detailed for a mile in each direction, and then a vague sector called 'Further out in La Crosse' or 'North La Crosse' or 'Past the hospitals'; beyond that – wilderness, infinite wilderness. For the rest of us the infinite wilderness doesn't begin till somewhere past the moon. So for these people a great many real things that have real bearing on their lives go uncharted. If you had an Einstein here and you gave him one of these La Crosse maps to start with, he'd at least make it to Chicago – he'd be curious, he'd explore. He wouldn't settle for the map. So then you wouldn't any longer have an Einstein here. You'd have another Billy Verité to take his place, though, someone who doesn't have the wherewithal to make it across the river. So again it comes down to leaving and staying; it's this selective outmigration that defines the small city. It's not just La Crosse, it's all small cities – and small towns, too."

I wouldn't say I disagree with him. I would say . . . I agree with him. But sometimes I remember the good old days, the days I knew were going to be called the good old days even as they happened – which is what real good old days are. I was in a position I'm in no position to describe in detail, in which the money, though it wasn't much, came easy – it wasn't much, but it was enough to pay a cheap rent, to eat at Sabatino's or the Lunch Encounter whenever I wanted, enough for cigarettes and coffee. I slept as late as I wanted, took long walks, and knew a woman who let me lean back into her in the bath tub while I smoked. I was only obliged to be someplace for one hour a day, and only three days a week. I knew then they were the good old days – and they happened here.

In the movie *Johnny Guitar*, Sterling Hayden, caught

between the good bad guys and the bad good guys, delivers the following sermon: "There's nothing like a good smoke and a cup of coffee. You know, some men got the craving for gold and silver. Others need lots of land with herds of cattle. And there's those that got the weakness for whiskey and for women. . . . When you boil it all down what does a man really need – just a smoke and a cup of coffee."

Sometimes that's the way I feel, the way I feel in La Crosse. I have all I need here. I never run out of coffee, and the Joie de Gas is open twenty-four hours if I need cigarettes at three-thirty in the morning. I try never to fall asleep with an empty pack; I try to leave one in case I wake up. The woman starts her goddamn coughing maybe an hour after I've fallen asleep. Soon the pall it spreads on my sleep becomes intolerable, and somewhere deep inside me, where a tiny survivalist we'll call Sparky resides, I realize the healthy thing to do is get up and have a smoke, that last one. And try getting back to sleep with that hacking going on . . . So at three-thirty there I am walking to the Joie de Gas, where Margo Zimmer has my smokes and two books of matches on the counter before I'm through the doors.

"Another thing I like about *Johnny Guitar,*" I tell Margo, who loves movies (wood chips and movies), "is that they got Johnny *Guitar,* and the *Dancing* Kid, and they actually follow up on it. I don't remember exactly how it goes, but it's something like: 'Johnny Guitar, eh? So, you really play the guitar?' And Sterling Hayden says something like, 'Dancing Kid, eh? You really know how to dance?' So this showdown happens, the classic Western showdown, but instead of a shootout it's essentially the characters proving that they earned their nicknames. Johnny Guitar really plays the guitar, and plays it beautifully – it brings tears to Joan Crawford's eyes (for more reasons than one, of course) – and the Dancing Kid really dances. And they play it straight. If you ask me it's one of the funniest scenes in the history of film."

"And there's not even a plaque with his name on it," Margo laments.

What she's talking about is the way La Crosse refuses to honor Nick Ray, the director of *Johnny Guitar,* who was from here, but has been ignored by city officials since he drifted out of the Driftless Zone to make good, even though in all his movies you can detect the thematic tension between *drift* and *driftless.* Maybe it wasn't his betrayal – his escape – that turned his hometown against him. Maybe he simply walked off the map. And here again I wonder what it was about our land that made the glaciers decide to avoid it. What does it mean that the ice refused to come? What did the ice know?

Earlier in the night, around nine-thirty, I look from the window of apartment 414 at the Cass Street Bridge, wondering over how all this Spleen business got started and how that bridge seems to have nothing to do with anything else that happened, knowing very well that it does. I can't make sense of it. What is it with that bridge? What manner of dissemblance does this false symbol bear? Lafly leaped and lived and there he was so long after, early in the day, walking down Cameron, across the street from me. I was in no mood to talk to him, but like most schizophrenics he won't tolerate people pretending they don't see him.

I threw my arm up grandly and called, "Lafly Junior!"

I crossed over and he came to the curb to meet me.

"I heard about your fall," I said.

He laughed a little and said, "Yeah."

"It was a prodigious feat of swimming," I said, trying to keep it matter-of-fact. "I'm glad you made it."

"Thanks."

"What're you doing now?"

"Working at a car dealer."

"Doing what?"

"Washing cars," he said, chuckling a little irony into the exchange.

"I quit doing shit work when I was thirty-four," I told him.

"I'm twenty-nine now."

We stood silent a few moments, wondering when we'd quit looking off to where no one had any ideas.

"I better go, then," I said finally.

So there he was, same as ever, unescaped and thorazined, his happiness and sadness blended together by science, so that there's no point to his having jumped, nor to anything that followed. I watch the yellow lights waltz in pairs along the bridge, disappearing into the mist. Now and then a semi from the brewery starts across, and it, too, disappears. I listen for a splash, but all I hear is a remote urban humming, faint under the plaint of a nighthawk. Between buildings softened by the thick mist moths live their absurd looping lives out in the skirts of doomed light. There is nothing else, nothing but the interiors, scattered isolate interiors, where lives have arrived leaving room for the moths till the outbreak of a blinding tomorrow. There is not enough light. I look back to the bridge for all the disappearances, realizing that if I don't get out soon the coughing will start up and it'll be me on that bridge.

I go to McDonald's for a smoke and a cup of coffee, and on the way something cheerless in the late summer air finds purchase in my lungs and I can't imagine what it's like to be unhappy – even here, where there are days when a cloud of some vague pain settles on the city, and people walk around with their ears stretched back, their faces tightened into grimaces that appear barely capable of leaking pathos from one stranger into another. I can't imagine more than that a better place exists; I can't imagine a reason to be there in that better place instead of here, where my cigarettes are, where my coffee is. If only my demographer friend could see me now. But when I get to McDonald's, as usual the only empty table is directly across from the Parasite Lady, who's got her blouse well-buttoned this time so that the only bits of the little half-tyke showing are her two feet, her two little angel feet, her two little five-digit arguments that one is either nomad or parasite. Looking at the little feet, dangling as from a corpse hung behind a curtain, I'm reminded of the scene near the beginning of *Kiss Me, Deadly,* after Cloris Leachman appears out of the night in front of Mike Hammer's car, setting off a desperate and mean chase after the great whatsit, the scene in which Miss Leachman gets strangled, the camera showing her only from the knees down. We see the death spasms of her lower legs and feet as she's lifted from the ground – the director apparently confident that what's glimpsed is more frightening than what's seen.

I saw that movie with Spleen, and we talked about that scene afterward, so perhaps I'm not out of line suggesting that I'm in part responsible for what was going through his mind when the bus pulled up to the Greyhound station. He must have been compelled unconsciously by the stiffening of the Sneering Brunette's leg to think back to the moments just after she said to him, "I've moved a lot since then," and he replied, "I've moved once," for he was trying to understand the flux of perception as it pertains to the sporadicity of love, and why the inability to determine truth does not always make arbitrary decisions tolerable – for it should, he figured, unwilling to decide that it wasn't his problem, that since in smaller doses truth exerts itself always in rapid flux, it's ill-aligned with the much grander and indecipherable slower flux of the universe, and so the potential justification for all malaise, even physical, is the frightening suggestions of brief glimpses – just like in the scene in *Kiss Me, Deadly.*

Call it a coincidence, but *I* showed Spleen the movie, and *I* was the one who brought up that scene and all this glimpse business (all right, that was later, perhaps much later, but when events are close enough that they can foist their unbearability off on you, you need to appropriate a portion of the blame in order to stand it) – and had Spleen not been thinking thusly he would've had time to get the hell out of the Volare when Billy Verité spotted Richie Buck lumbering off the bus and into a cab, and said, "We gotta roll," pulling out of the lot behind them.

The black undercover cop pulled onto Cameron behind the Volare, trying to fishtail the car, then to Stratton's horror braked abruptly and slammed the car into park.

Stratton, staring after the back end of the Volare, could not immediately express his astonishment.

The black undercover cop turned to him. "Wouldn't it break?"

"What?" Stratton watched the Volare, on Fourth now and heading south, change lanes past the Dance Building. His general stillness reflected no more than his physiological confusion as to how to panic.

"Wouldn't it break?" the black undercover cop asked again.

"What the fuck are you – look, look, we lost them, they turned off somewhere, must've been Market. Let's go!"

"Wouldn't . . , it . . . break."

"Wouldn't what break? Goddamnit, the man's a murderer and we're letting him get away!"

"The bratwurst. Wouldn't it break?"

"Oh, Christ – that? No. They were cooked. They were cold. They'd been in the refrigerator . . ."

Stratton breathed in, looked to the back of his eyelids, and let his frustration out his nostrils.

"Jesus, man, a good cop has to be objective. When he's on the job he can't be thinking of his or her personal life. You know that."

"You're right. I'm sorry."

"It's okay, buddy. We'll pick up the trail later. It's over – let's go get some sleep."

"Nothing's ever fucking over, that's what I can't stand," Deke Dobson was saying when Richie Buck cleared his throat behind him. Dobson turned from the window and saw Buck standing in the kitchen doorway. Within seconds Dobson expertly assessed Buck's capacity for mayhem, determining that it exceeded that of bigger men in lumberjack shirts who hadn't scared him all that much. Still, he declared by involuntarily thrusting out his jaw, he would not be rendered obsequious by the mere presence in his home of a force more menacing than he. He had too many years of leadership experience for that. What he found more difficult to control was the desire to stare at Buck's nose, which looked like a large apricot with two bullet holes in it.

"All right," Dobson said, forcing his eyes to wander from Buck's nose, "so you like to sneak in back doors. Fine. Welcome. I was just saying what I can't stand is how nothing is ever fucking over. You start something and you finish it and it's still not over. It goes on and on and on. Always some goddamn loose end running around somewhere. Know what I mean? Take your Nazis. They started it, we finished it, it still goes on. Nazis all over South America, Jews looking for them. New Nazis springing up everywhere, new Jews following right behind. I'm being hounded by Nazis and Jews. I can't make a move without it coming back to haunt me. I say something one day, some day three years later it's thrown back in my face. That's why you're here. I want you to end something for me. It's not going to end, it'll never end – that's what I can't stand – but I want you to end it anyway."

Even a nose like Buck's could decipher the decadent morning smell of moldering sheets that suffused Deke Dobson's house. In fact, Buck and his nose wanted nothing more than to get back outdoors as soon as possible. Buck looked at Dobson as Deke turned away from him to pull the drapes aside, looked at the sleeveless leather jacket that mentioned B.A.D. in yellowing letters, looked at the two long arms whose hairs and tattoos somehow seemed in a constant lag of torpor and alienation whenever their host moved, looked at the long black hair defenestrating from his scalp – unclean from an indoor neglect and studiously chopped so it would fall short of the jacket's letters – Buck looked at the man who had hired him and felt the familiar warmth of hatred gliding to his extremities. He hated Dobson the way he hated anybody who didn't shrink quickly enough away, and hated him again for being someone he wasn't going to kill. He hated Deke Dobson and wanted to kill him and couldn't kill him and so wanted all the more to kill him, fairly swooned with the squelchment of his desire to kill, and was finally forced, as he noticed himself edging murderously forward, to resort to recalling the memory of his father, who spoke the only words that still had the chance of temporarily soothing him: "Why do you have to hate, son? Why can't you just not like?"

That accomplished, he continued forward, hating the sunlight Dobson was letting in for not having the fortitude to refuse to die weakly on the carpet, a few feet from the window.

"I was followed here," Buck told Dobson.

"What," Dobson said, distracted.

"Who knew I was coming?"

"What? You were followed? See? Nothing's ever fucking over, even this. I have a bad feeling about this, too many loose ends. Things start and they multiply. Look at this: I move the drapes and a thousand particles of dust scatter. You think I wanted that? All I wanted was to move the fucking drapes. Same with the wheel, only worse. A man invents the wheel, one goddamn wheel, so he can roll it. Now the whole world is nothing but goddamn tires . . . And right now there are four goddamn tires parked across the street that I don't like."

Buck looked out the window.

"They followed me here, right up to the alley. Who knew I was coming?"

Dobson pointed to the corner of the room where the most recalcitrant of the previous night's darkness hunched about the stubborn slouch of a Lazy-Boy.

"I didn't tell nobody, Deke," said a voice that fell short of the sunlight.

Buck walked up to the chair, leaving Dobson at the window, and saw a small man with no eyebrows holding a quivering pigeon near his lap.

"Billy," Spleen said inside the Volare, "you might want to make yourself less conspicuous." It seemed to Spleen that when the drapes moved aside a man they couldn't see all that well could have a very clear view of them. He was trying to ignore the subtle cowering of the Sneering Brunette, who was staring at the passenger window. She hadn't said a word since Billy Verité mentioned Richie Buck and B.A.D., but now her entire body was stiff, not just her leg. For a split second Spleen's thoughts had wings and he wished he was the kind of man who could say, "Baby, you put the rigor in rigor mortis," but instead he was the kind of man who could listen to Billy Verité respond, "Hide in plain sight. Besides, he went in the back door – he'll expect anyone who followed him to be in the alley."

And Spleen was also the kind of man who could say with a straight face, "All right, Billy, this is your line, not mine. But we've got to go," and turning to the Sneering Brunette, who knew what was coming, he said, "Come on, let's go."

"Can't he drive us?" she asked, without bothering to conceal her panic.

"No can do, babe," Billy said. "Not when I'm on stake-out."

"Let's go," Spleen said.

The Sneering Brunette remained still, her face averted.

"What's wrong?" Spleen asked.

"It's cold out," she said.

"We'll walk fast. Come on, I'll walk you home first."

"Can I stay with you?"

Spleen felt an enormous sadness heave beneath his sternum. A mystery was thickening even as it expanded, and he was too tired to think about it. He closed his eyes. Fifty thousand moles were treading dirt far beneath the city, in constant scratching motions, burrowing frantic and nowhere, wondering if they could find their sorrow.

"Sure," he said.

"Her name is Nadine," the Fag With No Eyebrows told Richie Buck.

Buck held his hand open in front of Nadine, who hopped onto it when the Fag With No Eyebrows nudged her feathery hindparts.

"You don't have to be afraid. She won't hurt you. I found her injured and nursed her back to health. Now she's tame – a tame pigeon."

Buck's menace appeared to lift. He stroked Nadine's back with his finger. Nadine looked up at him with one guileless eye.

"We were going to be on TV, on Channel Eight. We had the interview set up, but then Deke said I had to cancel 'cause I couldn't leave the house. That means no network talk shows, either. She never tries to fly away. She's tame."

"Who followed us?" Buck asked Dobson as he leaned over Nadine to give her a peck on top her head. Nadine shrugged her shoulders.

"Wait," Deke said, "I don't fucking believe it."

Deke's nose was pressed against the windowpane.

"I can't – that's my woman. It's her! Come here. Who's that asshole she's getting out of the car with? Come here, goddamnit!"

The Fag With No Eyebrows hustled over to the window.

"That's Spleen."

"Who the fuck is Spleen?"

"I don't know – he's Spleen."

"Well, what the fuck is he doing with my woman?"

"You kicked her out, you told her – "

"I didn't tell her to go out and fuck some guy named Spleen."

Buck, gently stroking Nadine, walked up to the window.

"Who's that behind the wheel?"

"That's Billy Verité," Dobson said, "he's harmless. He didn't follow you, he brought my woman here so she could show me her new boyfriend. You see what I mean? It's never over. Look: the son of a bitch looks like a Nazi. It's like a birth. Something happens it's like a fucking birth. It lives its own life and before it dies it gives birth a thousand times. I can't fucking stand it. That bitch . . . What'd you say his name was? Spleen? . . . See? He's leaving."

Indeed, Billy Verité, having glimpsed the form of the

[64]

fugitive Richie aka Buck in the window, realizing his cover was blown, had decided it would be best to drive away.

"Richie," Dobson said, feeling a sort of familiarity one does before a big man stroking a pigeon, "sit down. I want to tell you about a man named Frank Barlow . . ."

Frank Barlow had simian arms, a beard he trimmed so that his face retained its pear shape, and a paranoia so grand it precluded all insight into the nature of the danger he was truly in. Had he the least inkling, he would not have been knocking on Spleen's door late that afternoon with somebody else's trouble on his mind.

"Frank," Spleen said when he opened the door.

"Spleen," Frank responded, "you're naked, and you have a tuft of hair above your pecker."

"Make coffee," Spleen said, shutting the door. "I need a shower."

Shortly after Spleen had shut himself in the bathroom, a voice slunk like an alley cat out of the bedroom. "Spleen?" it asked.

Frank Barlow, standing over the stove, glanced at the bathroom door and then quickly toward the bedroom doorway.

"No," he said, in a loud conspiratorial whisper. "No, it's me – Frank. Frank Barlow."

"Frank Barlow?" the Sneering Brunette cried out.

Barlow went to the bedroom to look at the face on the bed.

"Jesus H. Fucking Christ on a Hardroll – look who's hiding in Spleen's bed. Does he know you're in there? Better yet, does he know who you are?"

"I didn't know you knew Spleen."

"I didn't know *you* knew Spleen. I bet Spleen doesn't know you know me. I bet Spleen doesn't know how you know me. I bet Spleen doesn't know you know I know you know. Does he now? No?"

"Frank, Deke threw me out a month ago."

"Does Deke know what you know and I know and Spleen doesn't know?"

"I don't know. He might. We were at his house this morning – "

"At his house? You and Spleen paid him a social call? Holy Virgin Mother on a Buttered Slice of Bavarian Rye Bread, this is bad. B.A.D. bad. Bikers Ain't Drunks, Bikers Are Dumb, Brunettes Are Dangerous, Buddies Are Doomed, Beat A Dead horse . . . Christ Almighty I walked into a den of vipers."

"Nest," Spleen said.

Barlow turned around. "Do you know who you got coiled in your sheets?"

"Did you make coffee?"

"Spleen?" the Sneering Brunette gently interposed, "I need to explain."

"I need coffee."

"I'll make coffee," Barlow said, following Spleen back into the kitchen. "You go in there and let her explain. Say, does Roman know you use an aluminum coffee pot? That's who I came here to talk to you about, Roman."

Spleen, wearing his damp towel, elected not to return to the bedroom, sitting at the oval formica table instead.

"Spleen?"

"I need coffee. Why don't you come out here?"

"You did Gerard a real favor letting him take your place at the Red House, Spleen. Roman's gone berserk. The other morning Gerard heard him pacing the hall outside his room chanting, 'Kill him . . . Kill him . . . Kill him . . . ' He's wedging his door shut at night now."

Barlow swung his head at the Sneering Brunette, who had emerged wearing her own towel. "But I see you got your own problems."

"Thanks for putting in a nice word, Frank," the Sneering Brunette said. She sat down across the oval formica table from Spleen

"Frank," she continued, "we've all got the same prob lem."

"No, that's mathematically impossible. You're *part* of my problem."

"That's not true, and it never was."

"*That's* not true."

The room lapsed silently into the evening. Spleen looked out the window, the Sneering Brunette looked at Spleen, Barlow leached aluminum into the coffee. No one spoke again until Barlow brought three cups of it to the table. "Let's drink it black, what do you say?"

"Fine," they muttered agreeably.

"It's like a sauna in here, but you won't get me into a towel, not with these tits. Spleen, you know the Fag With No Eyebrows?"

"Sure, Frank, who doesn't?"

"You know he was in jail, then, right?"

"Right."

"Well, while the pusillanimous partly pubescent pansy was behind bars, he was seeing a counselor. You know who

[67]

that was? Me. I counseled him. In all things. Gave him advice on all manner of worldly affairs. He was going to straighten out his life. Not go straight, but straighten a few things out. We used to call it getting your shit together . . . an odd phrase . . . but he had one big problem . . ."

Barlow turned to the Sneering Brunette, then back to Spleen.

"No, two – two problems. Her and Deke Dobson. Before the Fag went back to the big house, Deke got it into his head that he wanted to try a ménage au gratin or whatever they call it, two men, one brunette. Am I faithful to the facts thus far?"

"Yes, Frank," the Sneering Brunette said, with an impressive neutrality.

"Good. So he wanted to try a threesome and he recruited the Fag With No Eyebrows. I don't know what the deal was – she might. Five bucks, puffy little promises, some of her underthings – "

"Christ, Frank."

Spleen's silence was that of a man who had yet to determine which of the lives he thought he had recognized he was expected to bring to bear on the events imposing themselves on him. Things were happening fast, yet the days were longer than ever; and recognizing the paradox was no more rewarding than trying to spank a conundrum with a handsaw.

"I can't tell you how it went," Barlow went on, "but I'm sure you understand the implications for a man of Deke Dobson's caliber and professional standing. Imagine if anybody in his gang found out about it. They'd rebel. They'd pound him silly. They'd *maul* him. He'd be an object of ridicule. They'd run him out of town. The leader of their gang a faggot. Imagine how awful. So what does the evil motherfucker do? What does the chickenshit cocksucking coward do? He tells the Fag With No Eyebrows that if he ever tells anybody about it he'll kill him, or have him killed. If Deke even suspects the Fag of such folly he'll kill him. So big deal, right? Just a little intimidation. Well, the thing is – did you ever read about Dobson's brush with the law?"

"The guy who tried to leave the gang."

"Right. Took him down into the basement, his basement – and *hers* – took him into *their* basement, had his lieutenants pistol-whip him, got his fingerprints on the gun, the same gun they were cracking him in the head with, and told the renegade that that gun would be taken to Milwaukee where a 'nigger or two' would be shot with it so that if he elected to leave the gang he'd be turned in for murder. It was a tactical mistake. The guy was more afraid of the murder charge than the wrath of Deke and he turned rat. The mechanisms of the law went into full operation and Dobson got probation. Two full years. And the amazing thing – the guy has balls, I admit – is he showed the newspaper stories to the Fag With No Eyebrows to prove that he meant business – see? He shows the Fag the very way to send him to prison for a very long time, counting on the Fag being too scared to see it, which he was . . . You're the last person in the world who still boils his coffee, Spleen, you know that? . . . Should I tell him the rest?"

The Sneering Brunette looked up from her coffee at Frank Barlow and smiled. At the sight of the curve of her sneering lip, Spleen felt a spasm of regret.

"I've only known him for twenty-four hours, Frank,"

[69]

she said. "You're not breaking up the romance of the century."

"Very well, then. I'm glad at least the romance of the decade is over. And what a romance it was, Spleen. You probably don't know that she worked at the County with me, but she did. That gave her access to the Fag With No Eyebrows, secret access, if you know what I mean. That meant she could aid and abet her loved one in his extortions. Too harsh a word? Sometimes silence is worth a lot more than money. She could also give advice and counsel to the Fag. And in doing so she discovered that the Fag had spilled the beans, that he had, through my – my what? – anyway, that I had arranged for him to speak with ace reporter Fingers Furlong, who said that all he had to do was file a complaint with the police and the story would be headline news and Deke Dobson himself would be sent to an even bigger house, and for a longer time. So she delivered a personal letter from Deke Dobson, who always has friends in the county jail, and suddenly the Fag With No Eyebrows has refused to see me and now I have goons in leather jackets following me on the street, afraid to touch me because it's a public matter, but hoping to scare me so I'll shut up, because Deke knows I know everything and that I'll tell anybody who'll listen that he's an extortionist who sleeps with men. Did I leave anything out? Did I tell any lies?"

"No, Frank," the Sneering Brunette said dispassionately. "It's all true." She turned to Spleen. "It's all true, Spleen."

Spleen felt like a man who didn't understand the game of chess. An heroic but decidedly petty struggle was taking place, pieces being moved before him without his having the slightest idea how any of them operated, nor what any of them was worth. He could sense the overall logic of causality at work, yet was unable to comprehend the shifty presence of contingency between particular events. The missing link was undoubtedly his own involvement. He felt as though he had managed to doze through an opportunity for heroism, that he was now being provided the merest glimpse of that opportunity, irretrievably gone, that he was witnessing the gentle mockery that fronted for every secret which men risk their lives to become disappointed in. He looked at the Sneering Brunette, saw her displaying the grandeur of her resignation for him, saw that for the moment there was nothing false in her, and knew as a consequence that there was nothing he could say to her.

"It's time for me to get dressed," she said.

"And not only that," Barlow said, "Roman's been having private tantrums. Gerard hears him breaking things in his room. The other day he came home to find the remains of Zirngibl's table, that wood one that used to be in the dining room, piled in the backyard. Sometimes he pounds on the bathroom wall while Gerard is sleeping. But the worst was the chanting. I want you to help me talk Gerard into moving out. I think Roman's finally beyond our help."

"Roman wasn't specific about the him the 'kill him' referred to?"

"No, just 'Kill him . . . Kill him . . . Kill him . . . ' The problem is Gerard's got a new girlfriend and he doesn't want to move until they can find a place together. But that could take a month or two, maybe longer. I think he's in too much danger to wait."

"Who's the new girlfriend?"

"That blonde who used to go out with the black under-cover cop. That's another problem. She dumped the poor bastard and he's taken it badly. Sometimes Gerard's over at her place and sees the guy in his car, halfway down the block. All night long. She gets heavy breathing calls, too – Well, Holy Flaming Genitalia of the Major Saints, will you look at her all gussied up!"

The Sneering Brunette was ready to leave.

"That was fast," Frank said.

"I'm sorry, Spleen. You too, Frank. Spleen, you better tell him what happened earlier. It could be true."

Spleen watched her open the door and knew she would-n't be the type to pause long enough to find out he wasn't going to say anything and then come scampering back with tears in her eyes, crying, "Oh, my Spleen, my Spleen." He knew that that kind of back of that kind of woman would walk out and never regard him as anything more than twenty-four hours of languid acquaintance with gleeful in-terludes and a close fit or a close call, a framing that being framed meant no more or less than anything else framed or that could be framed, a time that could easily do without the grief that seems the judgment on the concert of preter-natural love yelpings, the untainted orison of moans cast blindly in tandem out into that vast space again of mockery they chose wholeheartedly to forget together as if space were an illusion they could shrink from or wake up to never again in the solitude that drove them in the first place into arms every bit as bizarre, unwieldy, and ultimately in-effectual as their own, which they know/have always known and know each other knows by virtue of an inexplicable apperceptual wizardry they share, and know they share, and together watch their watching, so that a sort of palimpsestual delusion is every bit as likely as that one or the other or both will refuse to acknowledge every end they arrived at; and this they know so well that every corner they reach is another reason to end it all simply and painlessly instead of turning onto the next stretch which they know before turning can only be a replication of the last.

"Will you," Spleen said with such unpremeditated emotional mystery that the Sneering Brunette stopped herself as she was shutting the door and leaned back into the apartment, "will you," he repeated, "come back?"

In the second or two before she answered her eyes suggested to Spleen that she understood a great deal more than he would have guessed, and that she could shrug off layers of artifice at will – for the right man.

"Yes," she said. "Sometime later tonight."

"Boy," Frank Barlow said once the door was shut, "you are calling down upon yourself the wrath of the seven-headed snake-demon goddess. Sweet Rolling Gutter Balls of Moses you are consigning yourself to wander inflamed among the doomed and the damned – she will lead you down the dark path of – "

"Frank. I like her, Frank," Spleen said, before describing to Barlow the events that had taken place that morning, to which Barlow responded, "Well, Spleen, I'd say folderol, but I don't know what that means. So let's just say I say: *Balderdash!* What manner of tripe must needs this be? Whence came *these* scurrilous squidrompings? Fie! . . . on the whole turdswallowing ballydaphne. In other words: what are you saying, man! Have you gone mad? Are we to

[73]

live our lives out in the noirdreams of our man Billy Verité? Are we men who run from we know not what? No. We're men who need to know what we're running from. And I already know what I'm running from – the faces of my childhood. I've told you about them, haven't I? If not, more later. If these are some of the same faces, then, Dark Spleen, I romp, I run, like the godwind of the great and true fart of the original universe. But not before."

But earlier that morning, while Frank Barlow tossed in bed to the easy dreams of insufficient paranoia, Deke Dobson was planning his demise.

"... so you see, Richie, he must be eliminated. I've talked to you about the way nothing is ever over. It makes me sick. I have seventy men under me who look for me to do their thinking. These loose ends are not their concern – they don't see them. They couldn't see them if they tried. But they're all I see, they keep adding up, thousands of them. I can't fucking stand it."

"What about him?" Buck asked, shrugging a shoulder toward the Fag With No Eyebrows so that his hands could continue caressing Nadine. "He strikes me as the loosest end of all."

"I won't talk," the Fag With No Eyebrows said.

"No," Deke said, "he'll never talk. He understands me very well at this point. He knows I have long arms."

Richie Buck stood slowly and walked across the room to the Lazy-Boy. Looking down at the Fag With No Eyebrows, he said to Deke Dobson, "But you've involved me now. It's now my neck, too. I like it here, I like the Driftless Zone. I want to be able to – "

"The what? You like the what?" Dobson had come up beside him.

"The Driftless Zone. Where the glaciers never came. That's what they call it here, the Driftless Zone. I don't want little bald-faced boys running around who could identify me. He shouldn't be here."

The Fag With No Eyebrows could shrink no further away. He stared at Nadine, nestled happily in the loving hands of the man he feared was about to kill him.

"Please," he peeped, "I'll never talk. You can . . . you can have Nadine."

Richie Buck looked at Nadine. On her back was a little velvet carpet of gray. There was a violet band around her neck. He lifted her to his face, brushed her soft belly with his cheek.

"No," Buck said, "I could never take your bird away from you. I know you won't talk."

He kissed Nadine on the top of her gray head. He looked without guile into her guileless eye. He opened his mouth wide and closed his teeth on her neck, bit her clean through the neck, so suddenly that the last independent movement of Nadine's body was a lurch or a swell cut off by the squeeze of Buck's hand, and then a moment later a final collapse in on itself, the whole brief process like one last melodramatic superbreath. Buck turned the body upsidedown as he chewed so that the little blood that bled dripped onto the Fag With No Eyebrows, whose only reaction was a gape-mouthed terror, his lower jaws working mechanically, automatically, with the precision and stupidity of a piston. For the next few minutes, Deke Dobson watched with disbelief while Buck chewed, listening to the

[75]

sound of the bird's skull being mashed, a sound like nothing so much as the sound of a bird's skull being chewed by a very dangerous man with gray feathers and traces of pigeon blood on his lips.

After the final swallow, accomplished without water, Buck wiped his lips with the sleeve of his lumberjack shirt, and said, "He'll never talk."

4

I was glad she wasn't wearing her stockings over her head and holding a gun in her hand.

— Cornell Woolrich, *Mexican Weekend*

Is it safe?

Is it safe for a petty snitch who has no eyebrows to sneak out of Deke Dobson's house, where he is being detained by a barrier constructed of barbed wires of intimidation and electric fences of fear, and make his way to Spleen to warn him that Richie Buck has been offered an extra grand if he will include in his program of mayhem the breaking of both of Spleen's legs?

Is it safe for a weak little person who has just had the head of his pigeon taken gruesomely away to grow in his mind a conscience in the shape of that pigeon head that instead of cooing insists parrot-like incessantly, 'Go warn Spleen since it was you what fingered him, you little weasel,' and to then act on that conscience?

Yes, surprisingly, it is safe, on the principle of the second dead monkey or the first dead pigeon. This dead monkey business goes back to a boy named Sturgis who had a pet monkey that was invited with him to appear on a children's television show. The night before the show the monkey hanged itself from a tree in Sturgis's yard. (Suicide? No – too hopeful; the monkey just got caught up in its leash.) Everyone felt sorry for Sturgis and so he got another monkey – it's easy to imagine someone saying, "That boy's got another monkey coming to him" – and of course he was invited again to appear on the television show. This time he was extra careful. The night before the show Sturgis took the monkey to bed with him. In the morning he woke to find he'd smothered the monkey to death while he slept. It doesn't matter whether he rolled over onto it or simply held it too close to the breast – the emotional affliction cast by this story can only be spoken by a small boy with rocks in his mouth: it's dreshful.

If you don't know Sturgis, if you weren't there, you might ask: So what ever happened? Did he get a third monkey? Did he get on the show? But if you knew him, you'd answer: Who knows? Who cares? A guy who has one monkey hang itself and smothers the next one while he sleeps is finished. He recedes. He sits in a corner of the room without light, issuing the subtlest odor of slow moldering cells. He becomes dreshful.

Same with a guy who just had his pigeon's head eaten by a hit man, but only to this degree: he's got about thirty minutes. If he leaves and he's back in thirty minutes they'll never notice he's gone. If he's later than that, they'll notice, and they'll ask him where he was and he'll immediately break down, start blubbering, tell them everything – far more than they would've suspected – and then they'll kill him, gruesomely.

Is it safe?

No, I guess not.

Or: sort of.

Then why would he do it?

In the movie *Marathon Man,* Dustin Hoffman either knows nothing or doesn't know what he knows, so when Laurence Olivier, dental devices in hand, anaesthetic nowhere in sight, asks him if it's safe, Hoffman has no idea what to say.

Is it safe?

Is what safe?

Is it safe?

Is what safe?

Is it safe?

Yes, it's very safe.

Is it safe?

No, it's not safe, it's not safe at all.

Sir Laurence drills, Hoffman screams, Hoffman passes out, Hoffman doesn't talk. But he would have if he'd known what to say.

Olivier the mad Nazi dentist represents implacable evil. Hoffman strapped into a chair knowing nothing represents the desire to accommodate said evil. But what does evil want? What the hell does it want?

The Fag With No Eyebrows didn't know. But he was small enough to know that evil is even bigger than Richie

Buck, mightier than Deke Dobson, worse than B.A.D. Roman liked to say, "Please all and you please none." The Fag With No Eyebrows suspected that evil was all, and so he chose to please none. He snuck out one night and returned in twenty minutes. He went to warn Spleen he was in trouble and he got away with it.

Clearly then, trouble comes in all shapes and sizes. And you never know what it's going to do. Sometimes it skirts glum houses in dark night snow-relief like a shadow greedily devouring the substance it was skulked from, or like a conscience frantically searching for the chaos it thought it had to flee in the manner of a slick fun-loving fetus. But sometimes that's just the Fag With No Eyebrows, scared modestly witful, or enough to make him think the safer course would be to flatten himself against the houses of Spleen's neighbors rather than risk being spotted on the sidewalk looking over his shoulder every few steps, on his way like a prancing Cerberus to deliver a message and lead the way then back to the very bowels of insipid malice.

And sometimes trouble can take the shape of lips notoriously horizontal formed astonishingly circular in order to slide with a snail's snug ease down or up the penis of a man called Spleen while he sits sans thoughts of trouble, for he saw in their descent, those lips, he saw their troublesome sneer that said you will say yes to this trouble, as Spleen did in fact say yes to that trouble, which is to call trouble something epiphanous like liquid and a Spleen's yes something like an immersion, entirely different nonetheless from the illimitable wasteland of forgetting that but rarely occurs when two beasts forge a disappointingly licit bond in safe enclosures, for in this case one head is up here and one

down there, leaving Spleen as happily alone with his clarity
of thought and vision and memory as a man in a white cot-
ton suit on a rocking chair on a porch in the tropics at dusk
after a windless downpour, thinking least of all that he is in
a place that Spleen would call Ceylon, or Samburan, or
Ambon, a place where a word like commerce is meant with
the same eyes looking up at Spleen through a languid fall of
hair mysteriously sentient yet discreet regarding its terms of
disclosure, where a word like commerce is spoken through
lips the same as these whose sneer is acknowledgement
without necessity of invitation that what power there is to
be had has been had and relinquished so that a Spleen
might be delivered once, just once, to that place where
abundance rises up to swallow artifice, where regeneration
and decomposition mingle gently, as delicately as the wings
of insects making songs for the comportment of a man with
his own death, so that he may, in his rocking chair, be able
without hunger to imagine the parrot-feather odors of fried
plantain spitting under a red flood of Ibo chicken, or the
fresh-speared and brazen bulk of island boar roasting over
an Alfuro flame, or the nine lesser fruits abob in a restora-
tive lagoon of Palembang Punch, bobbing aside to make
way for the last little planet of mccchi melon that tumbles
niagric into your coconut-ladle, promising as it spins your
eternal life and that whether you are Spleen or not Spleen
does not matter, for such is this place of no forgetting that
all may be forgotten, and even a Spleen need not wonder
why it comes to mind that someone's in the kitchen with
Dinah, nor that he hummed such warning to the Sneering
Brunette, who smiled without interrupting her slavers and
smiled again when at the tapping on the door she met
Spleen's eyes and knew he would ignore it in the same way

and for the same reason, and she, too, mouth full, hummed, hummed low and soothing the same song, humming long after Spleen forgot Dinah in order to remember a time with a different woman when the power was his to relinquish, the woman, the excoriator, on her knees before him, desperately trying to reacquire what was lost when her own love vanished in the manner of a fart that in dissipating leaves behind only the afterknowledge of its egregious intent, a power he shuddered off like one would a tarantula that would then skitter heavily off into the woman's heart where it would not rest until she had the last words that Spleen would listen to with the unarmed and dull attention of a dog or a man in a white suit on a rocking chair in the tropics, who only knows what he's waiting for when a Sneering Brunette condescends to look doorward at the persistence of a tapping that apparently is impervious to light and silent scorn, looking over her shoulder and leaving Spleen's penis tottering like a coconut palm in a storm just as it accedes to the tremors it so joyfully suppressed, and looks back at Spleen's penis domed liquescent, feels where her hair captured a moment she realizes she missed with a regret immediately mollified by what Spleen can only figure is a great and rare spirit, and says, "Did you make a little spoojie?"

The tapping interminable, Spleen tucked, zipped, rose, and opened the door onto the spectral discountenance of the Fag With No Eyebrows, whose panic rearranged his warning into "I have to go, Deke paid somebody to break your legs," the last couple words spoken as he disappeared.

Spleen turned from the vacancy to declare to the Sneering Brunette, "I didn't make *that* little spoojie."

Thus an association was established that required an

[82]

immediate bath; and it was there in the bathtub that the Sneering Brunette, crushing thousands of little bubbles as she leaned back into Spleen, asked, "How do you make your living, Spleen?"

"Whose foot is this?" Spleen asked.

"It's mine . . . So how do you make your living, ex-farmboy?"

"I sponge off my twin brother. He's a success."

"Then it would be safe to say you don't have the money to flee."

Spleen plucked the soap from its porcelain perch and pushed the Sneering Brunette forward. He spiralled the soap in his hands to make lather, dropped the bar in the water, and began washing her back.

"I could get a ticket out," he said.

"But you won't, right?"

"Nixon once said, 'I could get a million dollars – but it would be wrong.'"

"Spleen, I know exactly what's happening. Deke hired a killer to take care of Barlow, saw you with me, found out who you are, and now he's put you on the list. Don't be too much of a man about this – these people will hurt you."

"Stand up."

The Sneering Brunette stood up.

"Spleen, you have to take this serious."

"I am."

"Not that – Wow! You must really like me."

"I've done this for no other animal, not even a horse."

"And a horse has never done it for me. Spleen, the Fag With No Eyebrows is practically Deke's prisoner. He took a risk coming here like that. You won't be safe unless you get out of town."

"I'd like to get out of town . . . Turn around . . . I'd like to get out of town, but there has to be a right way to go . . . Is this all right? . . . I don't know if I can explain any better. It's just that it seems to me I can't leave simply because the Fag With No Eyebrows came to my door and told me someone is going to break my legs."

Spleen had a point. He was not the kind of person who gets run out of town. He wasn't a heretic, a Jew, an intellectual apostate, a running dog, a reactionary, a Greek, a Turk, a Bulgarian, a sheriff, a gypsy, a con artist, a prostitute, a witch, a hustler, a gambler, a grifter, a dim-witted brute, a hobo, an adultress, a stool pigeon, a worshipper of Satan, a purveyor of child pornography, a filmer of snuffs, a flasher, a rapist, a pederast, a charlatan, a demagogue, a fallen priest, a levitating nun, a vigilante, a mad scientist, a carnie, a scab, a lone wolf, a rogue, a rakishly handsome womanizer, a faith healer, an imposter, a drag queen, a pusher, a mole, a traitor, a collaborator, a child-beater, an epileptic, a seer, an untouchable, a scapegoat, a mysterious itinerant farm hand, a contagious person, a quack, a fraud, a chiseler, a riff, a raff, a deserter, a bad actor, a peeping tom, a panderer, a beggar, a necrophiliac, a backslider, a sleazy nogoodnik, a pedant, a pissant, a moonshiner, a pirate, an inscrutable foreigner, a bigamist (or any other kind of heavily-armed Mormon) – Spleen was none of these types who get run out of town. Had he fallen into any of these categories, or been clearly accused of being, say, a chiseler or Turk, he would gladly have left. There's law and there's order, Spleen understood this, he accepted it as a way civilization kept track of itself; he was willing to acknowledge the implacable mechanisms set like omniscient robot dogs upon wayward manifestations of a still mysterious, autochthonous will to disorder. The problem was that Spleen failed to recognize the gloriously sterilized civilization at the heart of Deke Dobson's agenda, the tiny little city of the future of Deke Dobson's dreams that looked like a miniature replica of the very burg man had been marching toward for nearly three thousand years.

"All right," he said to the Sneering Brunette, "you can sit down."

"You want me to wash you?"

"No, I'll do it quick so we can get settled, maybe fall asleep before the coughing starts."

Meanwhile, Spleen's hands were moving like crabs along the bottom of the tub, trying to find the soap. Soon the Sneering Brunette joined in the search, which they abandoned after less than a minute in order to dry themselves in a state of distracted perplexity, watching the draining tub, expecting at any moment to see a white hump settle into view.

It never did.

Speaking of soap, Billy Verité once had a bar that had been carved into a pigeon. Back when he was driving cab full time, Billy drove a big man with a beard from La Vonne's Tavern all the way out to the Twi*Lite Motel. When they got there the man said he didn't have any money. "I just got out of jail," he said. Billy Verité was afraid that if he called the police, or even threatened to, the man would beat him up. "What can you give me?" he asked. The man, who didn't even have a bag with him, reached into his coat pocket and produced the pigeon, once a bar of white Safeguard soap, the kind Billy's grandmother had used. Billy had street smarts. He wanted that pigeon bad, but he pretended he didn't. "I'll take that for now," he said, "just to be a nice guy. But I'll expect you to pay the fare eventually. Here's a card. I'm number twenty-three – you can send the money to the office." And he had his pigeon. He was so happy he never wondered what the guy was doing going to a motel if he was broke.

Billy Verité took the pigeon home, and for want of a better place, put it in his bedroom on the porcelain ledge back of the toilet. He had no shower, thus no shower curtain, so whenever he bathed, which back then was every day, he could look at the bird. On the fifth day, as if engaged in an experiment to demonstrate the inexplicability of the basic and expected in human behavior, he left the tub to grab the pigeon, which was carved so expertly – except for the eyes, which were perfect – he imagined a subsidence of fluttering as soon as he held it in his hand. He cradled it, marvelling at how much like feathers soap could be. As to what happened next, it's not enough to blame it on nostalgia, even if he did wet the bird, smell it, and remember his grandmother; for he then rubbed himself with it, all over, and kept at it without ever taking his eyes off the pigeon for more than a few seconds, examining its features without knowing what he was looking for, without ever stopping to regard it as a thing capable of a constant state. It wasn't long before it had no distinguishable features at all, before, for example, the wings were impossible to tell from the belly – before it looked like a little bowling pin. He kept at it until it was gone, towards the end simply hastening its diminishment by rubbing it hard between his hands. Why?

Everybody knows why, even if they think they don't, even if they can't explain. Billy Verité didn't think he knew why, he couldn't explain it, but he regretted it every time he thought about it.

Detective Stratton was feeling a similar sort of regret, coupled with the uneasy befuddlement of one who would offer obeisance to the Elusive if only he could find it, on the day he finally tracked down Billy Verité. The afternoon was proceeding in malevolent fashion: as he was leaving the County building, fumbling for change so he could buy a cup of coffee from a vending machine on his way out, Stratton dropped a quarter. He could afford the loss, since he had more quarters. And he could have appreciated the irony if the quarter had hit the floor and rolled underneath the machine. But he couldn't stand what did happen, because he didn't know what it was. He dropped the quarter and it didn't land. He didn't hear it hit the floor. He didn't feel it bounce off his body. It wasn't in his shirt pocket, nor stuck somewhere on his overcoat, nor on one of his shoes. He jumped up and down a couple times and the quarter did not fly up off him. He looked around with a desperation that seemed to be mocking itself. A janitor was watching him, leaning on his mop handle. Stratton wanted to weep. How was he ever going to find Billy Verité if he couldn't even find that fucking quarter? "What're you looking at?" he snapped at the janitor. "I wouldn't know, sir," the janitor replied. "Clean the fucking floor," Stratton said, storming out of the building.

Right then and there Stratton decided he would have to rely on his instincts. He'd been wasting his time. Billy

Verité was never parked at the bus station anymore, and he had no fixed address. This tracking business was just the sort of thing Stratton would've assigned some asshole with less seniority if he were not moonlighting on the Sherri Holloway case, if he had some asshole to assign it to – if he had not turned rogue. He hated it; it was too far from the solution of the case. It was not what detective work was all about. He had gone to the County building to flip like an automaton through the Holloway file, but nothing in it told him where Billy Verité was. He was going to have to rely on his instincts, and his instincts told him to forget Billy Verité, to take a night off.

That's why, later that night, Stratton was at a table against the wall in the 3-Deuces dance club trying to keep a waitress from crying loud enough for anyone to notice by draping an arm over her shoulders, behind her bowed and bobbing head, and whispering with some urgency, "Would you fucking stop crying!" He hoped to impart enough menace so that she would not only stop crying, but would also continue fucking him, never forgetting to be too scared to blab to his wife. The waitress continued to sob into her hands until Stratton realized the situation called for a certain tenderness he hadn't the patience for. He threw off his arm and muttered "Christ!" with an exquisitry of disgust he had no time to be proud of, for the gesture sent him looking barward, where Billy Verité stood asking the bartender where his fare was. "I'll be right back, honey," Stratton said, getting up to follow Billy long enough to discover that he was driving a taxi. The Veil of Illusion had been rent. The universe in which Stratton was too stupid to call cab companies to verify his hunch that Billy Verité no longer drove cab was gone; in its place was a world in which Billy drove Saturday nights and Stratton would know precisely where to find him.

Cops and cab drivers are fraternal twins of the night, separated at birth, torn apart by sardonic fate. Mongrelized already by paternity, they've been raised by wolves and jackals in packs that have a hard enough time recognizing their own blood kin. Approach a cop or cabbie and, pointing to the other, say, "That man is your brother," and he will respond, "You are mistaken. I am an only child, an orphan." They arrive at the same watering hole, eye each other across it warily, ignorant of a common, indistinct morphology, and the unbidden primal understanding arises in each of them that the other is the enemy or he wouldn't be there.

The watering hole was the parking lot of the Joie de Gas, where taxis waiting for calls parked side by side facing opposite directions like mating worms, the drivers vying for moments of significance they sought to nestle in their languor. Cops parked next to the entrance. Inside they ate microwave hot dogs at stand-up tables, eyeing customers who passed by to use the rest rooms in a way they hoped would suggest an enormously demeaning indifference and at the same time instill in them the fear of an omnipresent authority. The looks they gave were important to cops. They liked to say things like, "I looked at him like, I give a shit," and, "I gave him a look that like to shrivel his balls." They had a knack for using relatively few words to say the same thing in a few different ways.

But Detective Stratton was undercover and off duty. Instead of going inside he parked his green sedan in the far corner of the lot, facing Cass Street, from where he could watch the cabbies come and go in his rearview mirror.

When Billy Verité finally pulled up, Stratton maintained a clever placidity of posture so as not to alert Billy's potentially weaselish senses.

Stratton felt better than he had in weeks. The worst of the legwork was over – and fuck the black undercover cop whose help he obviously didn't need. Let the obsessive bastard stake out his ex-girlfriend – who had committed no crime – while he busted his ass solving the greatest crime in the history of the city. As for the waitress, he figured he at least had her shut up for the time being. It was too nice a night to worry about how to prevent something he feared was going to happen all too soon. February was thawing and the city was glazed sleekly with the reflections of its nightlife on the wet streets. Clouds moved low, gamboling across the sky as timidly luminescent as the moon they veiled. The bellies of the noctambulos were giddy with the rustling of mysteries that slumber through winter. Stratton rolled his windows halfway down. He stretched and sighed contentedly. He may have made an involuntary noise.

If only the moment could have lasted. If only he were the only predator in the vicinity. But it shouldn't take a road atlas to figure that Richie Buck's first move would be to seek out Billy Verité, that he would tail him for several weeks, and that the presence of an undercover cop within a block of him would not go unnoticed. Fugitives are wary men.

It was an hour before Billy Verité got another call. Stratton was just retreating from the inanity of one of his self-conscious sighs when he saw Billy's cab move into the alley. This is going to be easy, Stratton thought, until he saw Billy turn the other way, toward Division, where the house Spleen lived in squatted irrelevantly across from the alley.

Billy wasn't going to Spleen's house; Stratton turned into the alley just in time to see that Billy was headed east. Little fucker, Stratton muttered, driving toward the feckless irony that Spleen's house represented in that Stratton looked straight at it and didn't know who lived there. When he reached Division, Billy's taxi was out of sight. Fucker's speeding, he said, and guessed correctly that Billy had turned onto Seventh Street. He allowed Billy a two-block lead until he saw the cab pull over at Seventh and Hood, when he pulled up within half a block.

It's easy to tail a tailer. Richie Buck pulled over a block behind Stratton, vaguely disturbed at the prospect of having to eliminate this interloper whom he was already striving mightily to not like. He was beginning to become haunted by Deke Dobson's weary diatribe about loose ends. He was being paid to kill one man and maim another, and it now looked as if he'd have to take care of at least two for free.

Billy Verité, for his part, was only circumstantially oblivious. He knew he was being hunted – he could smell it – but, as there was no place for him to go – he of the small map – he figured the best place to hide was behind the hunter, whom he was spending all his spare time trying to locate. Thus far his first and last problem was having no idea where to look. He needed to get a fix on this guy before contacting the proper authorities, who were themselves hard to locate. Stakeouts at Deke Dobson's – in disguise, of course, and in a borrowed car – had proven fruitless. Buck was apparently staying elsewhere, if indeed it was Buck and not some imposter.

In this race between hunters Billy's only objective disadvantage was having a highly visible position in public affairs. Once Buck found out he drove cab on Saturday nights, Billy Verité became a marked man. Thus far he owed his life to Buck's prudence. Buck spent weekdays plotting Barlow's demise, and followed Billy on Saturday nights in order to discover just such an eventuality as his being followed by an undercover cop.

After Billy dropped his fare off in a North Side alley, he found a green sedan blocking the exit. He was so sure that it was Richie Buck he was unable to get his car into reverse. He was relieved to see Detective Stratton pop spryly from the vehicle.

"Detective Stratton," Billy said cheerfully as he climbed out of the cab.

Stratton said nothing. When he reached Billy, he grabbed his coat by the collar and pulled him toward the back of Zielke's Corner Tavern in order to get Billy out of sight so he could do to him whatever it is cops do to make snitches talk. Halfway there, though, Billy's compliance failed him, giving way before an unhappy convergence of physical factors: Billy's coat slipped over his head so that his arms lost their mobility, plunging now blindly forward yet wanting to pull backwards out of the coat; and before Billy's upper parts could solve their dilemma, his feet arrived on an especially resolute shell of ice. Billy's knees hit the ice hard enough that he bounced, his legs then extending backwards in one determined spasm, leaving his chin to break the second stage of the fall. Meanwhile, Stratton continued pulling in brutish exasperation.

To Billy Verité's credit, he did not whimper, even when Stratton had him backed against the backside of the tavern, clutching his shirt at the neck, slapping him repeatedly on both sides of the face, fore- and back-handed for the sake of efficiency, and as if Billy Verité were no more than a little hysterical person.

"Where's Spleen!" Stratton shouted when he was tired of watching Billy's head swivel.

Billy let out a "huh?" so genuine it could not have been heard by a dog.

"Goddamnit! Where's Spleen?"

"Spleen? Why Spleen? I don't know – home probably."

"Where does he live?"

"Why? What'd Spleen do?"

"That's police business – where is he?"

"What'd he do?"

Stratton slapped him a few more times.

The word "welt" travelled like a silverfish through the evacuation of Billy's consciousness.

"You answer me right now, you ugly little bastard, or you're facing a charge of accessory to murder and aiding and abetting a fugitive. You think I'm going to let a little turd like you stand between me and the biggest crime in the history of this city?"

"But Spleen's not a fugitive, Detective Stratton," Billy said with bracing sincerity, like a boy who doesn't understand that his father has rabies. Stratton was compelled to listen. "Spleen didn't kill nobody. If you want a murderer I've got one for you, if I get the reward. He's an FBI Most Wanted Fugitive going by the name of Richie Buck, and he's in town right now because he's being paid to kill – "

Buck clubbed Stratton to his knees with the back of his fist at the same time he squeezed Billy Verité's neck with his other hand. Billy felt the kind of rarefied fear one does when what once was considered an implacable force is down on its knees stunned, groping about with numb fingers for the gun tucked into the back of its pants. Billy's eyes were still in his head when Buck saw what Stratton was up to and released him in order to subdue the frisky copper.

By the time Buck had the gun barrel pressed into Stratton's temple, Billy was gone, taxi and all. Knowing he was about to die, Stratton nonetheless experienced an absurd moment of delight at the prospect that a time would come when he no longer felt pain throughout his body. He was amazed, yet being a man of little introspection, allowed the moment to pass. More profane matters were at hand; he had to find the words to save his life.

"Wait a second. Wait. You're making a mistake . . ."

Buck waited. He waited to consider the consequences of firing a shot in a relatively unfamiliar and residential neighborhood. He waited because he was beginning to think it might be a better idea to dash Stratton's skull against the ground.

"You're here to kill somebody . . . You kill a cop and you'll have to leave town right away . . . You can't kill a cop and get away with it . . . There's a witness . . . He knows your name . . . Listen, you want to kill me or finish the job you came to do? I think we can work this out. I think we can all be happy . . ."

Every word Stratton uttered preceded the accompanying thought. He had no idea what he meant. He was inspired.

"What do you mean?" Buck asked, less from the instinct of the beast who toys with his prey than from genuine mercenary concern.

Stratton was beginning to understand what he meant. The steel against his temple was feeling warmer. He could see himself aching miserably in a warm tub. He could see his partner smiling again. He could see his wife moving as if in a shared dream, undisturbed by his future assignations.

"Let me sit up," Stratton said.

"We'll take your car. Mine's stolen."

Buck directed Stratton to the Island by delivering a series of terse lefts and rights. Stratton sought frantically to organize his sales pitch, giving no thought whatsoever to the gun in Buck's hand. He knew this was one felon he could not disarm. Force was out of the question. That left the willingness to be diabolical.

Once on the Island, Buck told Stratton to turn south on Bainbridge. They passed dredge yards and chemical tanks that were turning an eerie undersea green in the pre-dawn light. After the car rumbled over the railroad tracks, Buck indicated a narrow dirt road that led into woods.

"All the way to the end," Buck said.

The road ended gradually, becoming a trail that dropped listlessly into a slough. Stratton stopped when he ran out of room.

"Look," he said to Buck, "my partner and I can keep Billy Verité's mouth shut. He's our man, no one else listens to him. Right now he'll be afraid to go to the law anyway. When he sees there's nothing in the papers about this he'll know he's in trouble. I'll find him and he'll do whatever I tell him. I'll be sure he doesn't open his mouth while you're at large. As far as that goes, you can operate freely – I can make sure of that. You can do whatever it is you came here to do."

Buck's impassivity lulled Stratton into a sense of security. He paused, looking from the gun that was pointed at him from Buck's lap up to the nostrils on Buck's face that looked like bullet holes. His stomach lurched.

"Of course, you could just kill me now, but then you'd have the best cop in the city all over your ass, instead of having him – and me – on your side . . ."

"Besides not wanting to die, what makes you want to do me this favor?"

"I'm glad you asked. We would expect you to do each of us a favor. Something you might enjoy. What do you say? Interested?"

Richie Buck was so interested, Stratton drove directly from the Island – where Buck, mysteriously, remained – to the black undercover cop's stakeout perch down the block from his ex-girlfriend's house.

"How goes it, pard?" Stratton asked innocently as he intruded upon his partner's brooding surveillance.

The black undercover cop couldn't believe what he'd just heard.

"You've got exactly three seconds to get your ass out of my car."

Stratton looked at him with great affection.

"Just giving you the ritz a little bit, pard. I've got some great news for you. I'm about to make you a happy man."

"You want to make me a happy man?"

"I sincerely do."

"Then get your ass out of my car."

"I'd like to. I think we both need some sleep. We need to get moving on this Holloway thing . . ."

"He's in there fucking her right now and you want to talk to me about the Holloway case? Get your amazingly stupid ass *out* of my car."

"All right, pard, I'll quit – "

The black undercover cop did half a breast stroke, using his right arm, clamping his hand around Stratton's throat.

"Say pard again," he said, squeezing.

"Listen – amigo. Loosen up a hair. Listen: your troubles are over. You don't have to sit here anymore. Trust me, I've taken care of it. What do you think I'm so happy about. Now take your hand away."

The black undercover cop let go.

"Thanks. Let's go. I'll tell you everything over breakfast. You won't believe it. I'll buy you breakfast, we'll get some sleep, and tonight we'll go after Spleen."

"Spleen – line two. Spleen – line two."

Spleen awoke early in the afternoon to the eerie incantations of a female loudspeaker voice. He figured out fairly quickly that the Sneering Brunette was gone. She wasn't in bed, and he could see through the kitchen and into the bathroom from where he lay. Sometimes if the breeze was westerly and the window was cracked to draw cigarette smoke out in the direction of the cougher, Spleen could hear the loudspeaker from the car lot a block and a half away on the corner of Fourth and Division, across from the Dance Building. The woman probably had not said Spleen at all; it was probably Gene, or Steve; but Spleen heard Spleen and he was stuck with it. Leaning up on his elbows he looked around, feeling like a soiled bedsheet. She was gone. Instead of leaping out of bed like a man of action he smoked a cigarette and monitored the diaspora of his thoughts. He watched where they went and so thought of the abyss, wishing it had the guts to show itself, to materialize or dematerialize as an authentic black chasm beside his bed. He realized, though, that all he had encountered thus far on this unaccountable afternoon, this desultory morning – the voice, his bedsheet, his skin, his brain – would immediately be sucked down into it, and he knew it so well he realized that that was precisely why it had no need to reveal itself. The cigarette succeeded in spreading the miasma throughout his body. He felt ill and hungry and knew he was far from having the energy to attempt a recovery. The future he saw was no further away than his bathroom; and it was as bleak and milky as belated self-awareness; it was an expanse of banality under a flickering low-wattage fluorescent bulb.

He lay flat again on the bed. Somewhere in the distance the distance bent into the abyss. He smoked another cigarette. When he stubbed it out he thought of the Sneering Brunette. He had no idea where she was, when he would see her again. He rolled toward the wall, pulled the sheet over his head, and encouraged the dull widening of his being by masturbating sluggishly.

part two:

when in doubt

5

Leave that black slip on, dance just like you
  did last time
Leave that black slip on, dance just like you
  did last time
I'm so glad your plans for leaving fell
  through just like mine

— Greg Brown, "Ballingall Hotel"

I'm not ashamed to admit that sometimes I still have to earn my living driving a cab (the best old days are gone), nor will I excuse the company I keep. It's true that sometimes before Billy Verité retired I'd be parked at the Joie de Gas and I'd see him coming and pull away before he got to me. Other times, though, I was, well, not grateful for the company, but I bought him breakfast at Sabatino's a couple times. There were other drivers, too, and I called them brothers – even those who referred to me as "that asshole," like Joe Kronski, a man stronger than a gorilla, and somewhat less sagacious. I caught him stealing one of my calls one time and challenged him over it at the office. He said he wanted to step outside so I followed him. Instead of charging me he picked up the picnic table next to the soda machine, lifted it over his head and slammed it to the ground. Then he approached me. I grinned and said, "Maybe I got it wrong." He respected my ability to capitulate without fear, and quite naturally came to hate me for it. But he never stole my calls after that night. I didn't hate him, not even as a plaything I could manipulate without personal gain, but now and then I had occasion to outwit him in such a way that he could suspect a universe existed that excluded him; and when he vaguely connected that universe with me, he was able to hate me all the more. Kronski drove more often than any other cab driver, every night if the company allowed. He had a slovenly wife and two brutish children who ran through his house tripping over soda cans that the wife used for ash trays. I often saw him in the afternoon long before he went to work, parked in the supermarket lot eating hot dogs for breakfast. Escape would never be a question for Kronski, for he found his paradise wherever he could bring himself to bear on circumstances eager to acknowledge their own lack of initiative.

If I irritated Kronski at times, if I could sometimes insinuate demonic notions into his paradise, he also had weapons, for it was impossible to avoid noticing that our very different habits of outlook and desire brought us to the very same place, waiting for calls in the parking lot of the Joie de Gas, where for the moment our concerns had been winnowed into the same trough. To make matters worse, the next cabbie to pull up would be the Swede, who had been at it for twenty-five years and always made more money than everybody else, yet never seemed to give a damn about it. Whenever I expressed the least fiscal anxiety to the Swede he'd tell me the same thing: "You're not seeing the overall." He got that from Hal Holbrook in *All the President's Men*. The Swede first saw the overall when he was a young man just out of college. On a particularly vivid acid sojourn he went to the north of India to see the Buddha, who instantly granted him bodhisattva status, instructing him to go back among the people and drive them from place to place, to be wise and humble before them, courteous and oblique, for they would give him money. He would turn with the wheel of life, but he would always be apart from it. He was saved. The Swede was a sane man, intelligent and as wise as the Buddha expected him to be. He, too, would never escape, he would die as a cab driver, even if he had the smarts to move on to greater things. He would tell me that if I only could see the overall I'd see that he already had escaped; and that I had escaped, too – we all had, if only we realized it.

So I could sit at the Joie de Gas in between Kronski and the Swede, Kronski eyeing me surreptitiously, doing his damnedest to make me think he was on to something, pretending to write cryptic notes on the back of his call sheet, delivering encoded messages to the dispatchers, practically swallowing his microphone in an effort to make me think he was being furtive, the dispatchers usually too lethargic to respond, occasionally modestly aggrieved, asking, "What are you trying to *say*, Joe?" and later Joe going so far as to imagine the sudden irruption of an idea that was out to conspire with him to betray me; and the Swede, slouched in his seat, looking up between the night clouds to a void he was certain he had the measure of, in all humility oblivious of the wobbling scaffoldings supporting the mundane world, scaffoldings the rest of us held up with our shoulders, our feet perpetually slipping as we swaddled our tiny fears and wondered how we managed so much of so little at once; I could sit there between these two and begin to sink into the driftless zone where escape is posed as a false question and equilibrium and the void are one, where desire has the same weight as anxiety and the voices of my brothers and the pocket change of my fares, where the totality of a city's perversions equals the sum of its ecstasies and moments of beauty minus the corridors of peace that run parallel to our forlorn conceptions of them, but I know that just as I begin to advance toward my bleak acquiescence, my adopted paradise, Arbogast will pull up in his yellow and black cab and he'll invite me in, tell me how much money he's making, how he needs a guy like me to run the show during his day shifts, how I've got to quit working for the enemy if we're ever going to get out of this town again, if I'm not to end up like one of these other guys, like Kronski, who works and sleeps and eats hot dogs, anything to keep away from a wife he can't live without and kids who aren't old enough yet for him to beat up, or like the Swede, who still can't get over the effects of a bad acid trip he took twenty-five years ago, or Billy Verité, who has a permanent crease in his left gonad from wearing his pants too tight. And I'll go off with Arbogast, and I'll manage his upstart rival company because he's the only brother I understand. He met a French woman in Benadorm, Spain, years ago and they had a nice night and all he wants to do with his life is get it back there, to

Benadorm. So he quit the only cab company in town to start his own, intending to drive rogue for a year, keep all the money, and take off; but one thing led to another and before he knew it he had a fleet, had gained seventy-five pounds, was smoking too much, and was always planning to escape in a few months more, sell the company for thirty grand and take off . . . I knew he'd never leave, five years having passed, yet as long as he didn't admit it to himself I could join him in his delusion – together, without stopping, never taking our eyes off tropical horizons, we could go nowhere.

It's an easy delusion to maintain when you can determine empirically that no one else is going anywhere, and that they're paying you for that privilege. At night I took my customers to bars and later on took them home again. What they did during the day was none of my business; all I could be sure of was that they needed to be stupefied in order to go through with it – or, when I'm feeling especially susceptible to a fleeting fondness for the human spirit, I figure they needed to squelch the perhaps primal and frightening unbidden desire to move on. And if that's true, if they were trying to establish in themselves a balance between fear of the unknown and a vestigial urgency pressing them some kind of onwards, then it could be that the cab driver is the saint who keeps them moving, providing them their last link to their selves, keeping them nomads. I can't think of a better reason for them to go from place to place – and for me to take them there – not after becoming a day driver and seeing where they go. No one can convince me that Edith Zimmer, Margo's aunt, really needed her hair done twice a week; or that the Colonel needed to visit the Eagle's Club three or more times a day; or that Margo herself went to the Joie de Gas five times a week just for the money. I'm not unaware that the weakest of the three examples is the last, the fare who takes a cab to and from work, yet I insist upon the possibility that the entire economic structure of our cities is an elaborate, if inadvertent, concoction designed to keep us moving, to forestall the final betrayal of our selves, the final settlement/dissolution/decay that has long been desquamating into our destiny. And if these may be taken as the fallow ravings of a once misfertile mind I ask only to be called as foolish as the first hominid to conceive an unintelligible intelligence beyond – that it be understood that occasionally a man needs an idea like he once needed the gods, that when a fare has a load of shit in his pants and the cab driver is forced to speed along the swamp road between the North Side and downtown with his head out the window he might need at least at that particular moment to feel that he's doing it for a good reason.

Other than the smell, the worst thing about the incident was that it happened at the end of my shift. I'd been driving since six in the morning and the call came in at about five-thirty. I fault no one's intentions; the fare was from the North Star Tavern on the North Side all the way back down to the Snakepit at Fourth and Division, the same intersection as my apartment building and the car lot. The dispatcher was giving me a good seven-dollar run to end my day.

It was early in the summer, the time of year I find most interesting in the olfactory sense. The various fresh odors of spring mingle with the advance odors of decay in all combinations, the bitter scents of life with the sweet decantings of death, most of the smells subtle and expansive as expensive perfumes. All this to say I drove to the North Side with my windows down, content to breathe in the cooling air until my stomach tingled with the anxiety that remains after not only the past is forgotten, but all its implications for the future as well. In short, I was happy, and remained that way even after I entered the bar, which was dark and smelled as it did all year of foul liquids long soaked into wood.

My fare was an old fellow named Earl, who resembled a bowling ball, and who never until this time had failed to mention that he was a hack back when you could go anywhere in town for a quarter. I was glad to see him, drunk though he obviously was; he never caused the least trouble and always managed to tip around a dollar. For as long as I'd known him he'd lived at the Snakepit, a notorious boarding house that took in mostly alcoholics who still liked to drink after their brush with Alcoholics Anonymous. They were generally good-natured drunks who'd been beaten up so many times they'd developed the habit of taking care of each other to some degree, doing what they could to prevent each other from getting kicked in the head any more than necessary. In nice weather they liked to sit around in lawn chairs hooting at the traffic on Fourth Street, and as I helped Earl off his bar stool I could already imagine a couple of them finding some way to get Earl to a comfortable spot.

I don't know when exactly he shit his pants, but I didn't notice a thing until I had made my U-turn and was headed back south. If the ungentle hand of a mean-spirited deity had ripped off my head just then and deposited it in a cesspool I could not have been as demoralized as I was when I was forced to reckon with the mess Earl had made. My first instinct was to turn back toward him – he was in the rear, passenger side – to release my disgust upon him like a plague; but he responded to the opening salvo of my fury with an infantile blubbering that quickly degenerated even further into a giggling punctuated by the chubby fist he kept rubbing across his mouth. I jerked my head away and thrust it out the window, at first unconcerned with the impression I offered, wanting not to return to a semblance of my previous mood, rather only to retrieve the atmosphere that had made it possible; but soon was aware of the spectacle I made and became even more angry, wanting to shout out to the cars passing in the other lanes that I was only doing this because that fat son of a bitch in my back seat – a grown goddamn man – had shit in his pants.

Earl and I bisected the swamp in that fashion, me with my head boring into the odors of summer, my lip under my front teeth to suppress the curses I knew would be received by the city's wilderness with an impassive scorn, Earl back there demonically oblivious.

Past the swamp I hit the first stoplights and an equilibrium was established that allowed Earl's stink to exceed the parameters of the cab and find my nose, while what fresh air made it past into the cab did little to alleviate it. The fleeting image I had of slamming my head into the steering wheel until I became unconscious beckoned like the most luscious of opiates; only by an uncommon and certainly unbidden resolution was I able to continue on when the lights turned green, leaving my self-pity clenched between my teeth. Spengler said the urban nomad can never leave the city because the city is inside him; he's condemned to wander burdened by the weight of a millennium of elaborate excuses for concrete and the repetition of automatons – the structures of the city recur in the way he thinks, operates his limbs, delegates responsibility to his senses; his home, his lost Atlantis, waits for him across a vast desert that cannot be crossed without the money belt that eventually breaks him down to die under the vultures, smiling finally at the paradise of his folly. It seemed to me as if for a few moments before I picked up Earl the city had released me – I was free to go, and in Spengler's sense, I did – but of course lurking inside me was a reception committee, waiting solemnly, without need for ceremony, for the city's return, which was accomplished by its agent, a man named Earl.

I made my way to the Snakepit, compressing such superstructures of agonized reasoning into a sort of rapture of futility: I have to get out of here, I have to get out of here, I have to get out of here – knowing I could not, at least that my escape was not imminent, yet no doubt deriving an insignificant satisfaction from repeating it in my mind.

I thought the worst of the ordeal would be over as soon as I arrived at Earl's home. He'd pay me and leave the cab, then I'd go home. But that last element of the transaction was designated to be the most torturous, a trial befitting Dantean conceptions of hellishness.

Put it in these terms: Take your victim, call him a cab driver. Have him pick up an old man with a low center of gravity. Have the man shit in his pants. Lead the cab driver to believe that the ordeal will end at the fare's destination (call it the Snakepit). Have several of the lumpen denizens of the Snakepit swilling whiskey on lawn chairs when the cab pulls up, a gallery of roguish spectators drinking to polish the edges of their menace. When the cab is stopped have the cab driver say, "We're here, Earl, that'll be seven dollars." Don't let Earl pay just yet, have him nod and giggle and refuse to move, even as the cab driver begins screaming at him, drawing the attention of Earl's cronies, who are immediately pleased at the sight and sound of this sideshow that's been delivered to them. Make them shout things like, "Hey, it's Earl," "Hey, Earl," and "What's he doing to Earl?" Don't let any of them get up to lend a hand. Have the cab driver try pleading with Earl, cajoling Earl, cursing Earl – for at least fifteen minutes that demonstrate for the cabbie an eternity because he sees absolutely no way to get Earl to give him the money and get out of the cab. Of all things, make sure Earl remains conscious. Liven it up a little, add some complexity, make the victim recall a phrase his father often used, run it through his mind, to wit: "like stink on shit," as in "I'm going to be all over you like stink on shit," and make it repeat in his mind, a feculent mantra: "like stink on shit, like stink on shit, like stink on shit," until it finally occurs to the cabbie to take Earl to the cops, when Earl finally pulls out two twenty dollar bills, forcing him to make a moral decision. Deprive the hack even of his moral triumph by having him decide not to take anything extra only because he's afraid of getting caught. Lead him to believe that Earl, having paid, will now leave the cab. Make Earl sit and giggle; don't let him move. Have the cabbie, in a rage, run around the car to Earl's door and try to pull Earl out of the cab. He won't be able to do it, not without Earl's help. Don't let Earl help. Have an extremely fat and cruel man wearing jeans and an unbuttoned blue workshirt walk out of the house just as someone says, "Look, he can't get Earl out of the car," and have him say, "What the fuck is he doing to Earl?" Make him suspect the driver of robbing Earl. While the driver continues to pull on Earl's arm, while Earl continues to giggle and wallow gravidly, while the lumpen in their lawn chairs hoot and cackle, have the fat man approach the driver saying, "Take your hands off him." Let him reach into his pocket for a buck knife that he opens and uses to clean a fingernail. Have the driver hear someone say, "You tell him, Bill," while he continues to pull Earl's arm. Have Bill, who is very, very strong, shove the driver with one arm so that he nearly falls, staggering several feet before finding his balance. Have all the boys crowd around and have Bill say, "I believe he stole Earl's money." Have the driver lose his temper, start hollering about how Earl shit his pants and even though he didn't charge an extra cent he could by all rights charge the twenty-five dollar cleaning fee. Let the only guy the driver recognizes stand forth; make him a big rawboned fellow, a dangerous man, but always fair with the driver in past dealings; have him respond to a nod from Bill by pinning the driver's arms behind him. Have Bill grab the driver by the hair, yank his head back, draw the blade of his knife through the air an eighth of an inch from his throat, then tap the side of the blade against the side of his neck, saying, "Earl's my friend," before kneeing him in the groin. Give the cabbie a moment to reflect, a very human moment – have him think that this couldn't possibly be happening. Let Bill say, "Go through his pockets, see if he has Earl's money," and, "Shut up or I'll cut you," when the driver begins to protest. Now, this driver's going to have a long life, at least another year or two, maybe more; it wouldn't do to have him lose all hope. Give him reason to believe it won't be worse next time; have something fortuitous happen. As the first hand thrusts itself into the cabbie's pocket, have Earl miraculously roll out of the cab onto his head, the rawboned fellow releasing the cabbie to go to Earl's aid, whereupon the cabbie rises to the occasion, blaming it all on Bill: "If you'd have helped him instead of trying to rob me, your friend would be fine right now, instead of lying there with a cracked skull. Now get him into the house and leave me the fuck alone."

That got me out of it, and to this day I'm not sure where it came from, for there were tears in my eyes when I said it and the shaking in my voice could not have been caused by Bill stomping his feet.

Back in the cab, I pulled out of the driveway, the crowd of derelicts circumscribing Earl, poking at him, Bill already back in his cave, disappeared like an arbitrary bloat of mischief. Before I could turn onto Fourth Street the dispatcher was calling.

"Thirteen. Where are you, Thirteen?"

"This is Thirteen," I told him, "I'm done working."

It may be true that these days you have to take things easy, shake them off like Robert Mitchum in *Out of the Past,* but I figured it would be easier if I went right home and ripped the door off my refrigerator.

"Need you for one more, Thirteen. Everyone's north, got a call south."

"Sorry, Mack. I was done a half hour ago. The nightmare, for me, is temporarily over. Goodnight."

"Thirteen."

I put my head out the window as I turned onto Fourth Street.

"Thirteen."

I could still hear it.

"Thirteen."

And I could still smell Earl.

"Thirteen."

They would hound me until my death.

"Thirteen."

"Yes, goddamnit, this is Thirteen and go fuck yourself, where's the goddamn fare?"

"Corner of Twenty-ninth and Trane. He'll be waiting outside. You won't regret it, it's a good run, all the way back down to Lafly's Antiques."

"Five dollars ain't enough right now. Ten-four, and, again, go fuck yourself."

"Thanks, Thirteen."

Mack dispatched with a certain manipulative equanimity.

On the way I stopped at the Texaco for some Lysol that did no more than make a porous wall between me and Earl. After a few blocks I stopped again, at an Amoco. I used a foam windshield washer to douse the seat and the worst of the smell was soon gone.

Spleen stood motionless at the corner of Twenty-ninth and Trane, looking toward the low sun. I looked at it, too, wishing it would go down and stay put until it came up with some better ideas. Spleen was wearing blue jeans and a green short-sleeved shirt with dolphins on it, untucked. When he heard me coming up behind him he turned, and I could see he had a crew cut and a two-day growth of beard.

When he got into the cab I was smiling like an idiot.

"It's you again," he said.

"Sorry about the smells," I said. "Hopefully it's mostly Lysol by now."

"Somebody retch in your cab?"

"No – an ex-cabbie shit his pants. But that's another story." It was either begin weeping, wiping snot on his pants leg, or try forgetting about it. "How about yourself – what're you doing out here?"

"Nothing in particular."

"Waiting long?"

"Yes."

"Sorry."

He didn't respond to that, so I pulled away from the curb.

"Going downtown, right?"

Spleen nodded.

I drove straight into the sun until I reached Mormon Coulee, where I turned north toward downtown. Spleen looked at me a couple times before deciding to go ahead and speak.

"You feeling better about that bird, the one that flew into your windshield?"

"You remember that? Christ, that was over a year ago. Yes, I'm over it. All I was really trying to get across was that I felt like shit for killing it. I'm no great bird lover, and it was only a sparrow, but you know, the way it happened . . . See, in truth it's more than just the killing of it, it's that careening glimpse of something live, seen only because it's about to die – and then the death drop, again just a glimpse – but the delay in between . . . But I'm not going to go into it again. It reminds me of a scene in the movie *Kiss Me, Deadly.* Ever see it?"

Spleen shook his head. As I described the movie I couldn't tell if he was listening or not. He looked ahead into traffic. I wondered if he was the kind of person who never got bored, having in him some mechanism that guided him into a different zone when he was sick of listening to someone (like me). To test him I drifted off in the middle of a sentence.

"Is that it?" he asked.

It could be that the same mechanism can bring the listener back at crucial moments.

"No, but I don't want to ruin it for you."

"Sounds interesting."

"Maybe we can see it sometime. You're friends with Barlow, right? We can watch it with him. He's a friend of mine, too."

"Sure."

It seemed important not to appear too eager, so I decided it was my turn not to respond.

Approaching the West Avenue lights I was trying to maneuver into the right lane when a blue van sped up alongside to prevent it.

"Fucking asshole," I said, braking to make room to slide in behind the van.

Spleen looked at me and smiled.

"So your last fare shit his pants, huh? How can you stand it?"

"I don't know . . . but something tells me that's the wrong question."

"What's the right question?"

"I don't know – Look: the asshole isn't even turning. Son of a bitch rushes to cut me off and he's going straight. He didn't even have to be in that lane. Fucking assholes . . . Maybe the question is somewhere in the very nature of the incident, a horrible event, though admittedly petty, and something that just rose up from the loins of human muddling or something. I mean to say it wasn't *devised* by anyone. I was put through torture – I had to drive with my head out the window, I was mobbed by thugs (yes, but let's not go into that), I was *tortured*, but nobody sentenced me.

No Idi Amin, no Suharto, no Kissinger. It just arose like a chancre from the flux of human activity. It's what you might call . . . life . . . There's a waitress over at Sabatino's. Whenever I go in there she says to me, 'How's the rough-and-tumble life of a hack?' The rough-and-tumble life of a hack. Well, I'm going to go there now after I drop you off and I'm going to tell her how the rough-and-tumble life of a hack is . . ."

"You're going now? Why don't you take me with you, I could eat something."

"You don't need to get to Lafly's?"

"I'm in no hurry."

We were coming up on Fourth and Division by then. The Snakepit lawn was vacant. There was no ambulance. I pointed to the Dance Building, up at my bedroom window.

"That's where I live."

"I live down there, a block and a half."

"I'll be damned. You hear the ambulance the other night?"

"No."

"Stopped right in front of the third house up. There's a lady there with an advanced case of tuberculosis or something."

"Coughs all night?"

"Right."

"I hear it."

"Well, an ambulance pulled up to her place and took somebody away. I figured it had to be her. So last night I got all relaxed, ready to stay home, enjoy the quiet, get a good night's sleep, and goddamnit if she didn't start up earlier than usual, about nine o'clock, worse than ever. Used to start around two, then gradually worked its way back to about ten. Now it looks like it's going to be nine. Christ. I know there's something to admire in all that, but there are times when it drives me nuts."

"I can usually ignore it after a while."

"Perhaps you're not as sensitive to apocalyptic foreboding as I am. If you ask me that woman spells doom . . . for us all."

Sabatino's was across the Mississippi, about a mile into Minnesota off the turnpike leading to La Crescent, a small town tucked in at the feet of the Minnesota bluffs. Spleen rode the rest of the way without speaking, looking slightly morose, as if considering whether or not his world were indeed coming to an end. The turnpike ran through swampland, and I was happy to again be under the illusion that I had left the city, even if I knew the odor of Sabatino's hash browns would soon bring me back to my senses.

The diner was a square building with a flat roof set virtually in the middle of nowhere. A car dealership was growing up around it; otherwise there was nothing for miles in any direction but swamp and the road leading out of it.

The waitress I was looking for wasn't there. Instead there was a bleached blonde with live hips and a bad complexion who wore her shirt untucked, and unbuttoned down to the kind of bosom that could give her an attitude in a joint like Sabatino's. But she wasn't going to ask me about the rough-and-tumble life of a hack.

She let us sit watching the last ice cubes melt in the water glasses before approaching our table.

"I was really hoping," I said before she could begin her interrogation, "to come in here and have my favorite waitress ask me about the rough-and-tumble life of a hack. Where – "

"Look, pal, you don't like the way I talk, get another waitress."

"You seem to be the only one here."

"There's others down the road, if you get my drift."

"Yeah? And how's the corned beef?"

"I'll have coffee," Spleen said.

"Me too, if it's still an option."

The waitress swished away gamely. I wished I could blame it all on sexual tension.

"Is it my attitude or hers?" I asked Spleen.

"Bad chemistry," he said, probably with some kindness.

"I've had a lot of trouble with that lately. What about you? I used to see you around all the time with that Japanese woman. Is that your wife?"

Spleen smiled.

"No. A friend. Nothing more. Ever."

"Bad subject?"

"It was once, but not with her or me."

"What about now? Are you with a woman?"

"Things are up in the air."

"I see. Ah, here's Lady Godiva."

"You can crack wise once more, pal. Just once, and then I have the cook tattoo your face with the waffle iron."

"Once more, huh? Okay, where do you want it?"

I leered at her chest for effect. She gave me a look like she wanted to knock my coffee onto my lap.

"Let's just get it over with," she said.

"Right. Look, I didn't mean to start trouble. I was just wondering about my friend. She never misses a Wednesday night."

"We don't know. She hasn't been in since last week. Nobody can get hold of her. She's not here tomorrow she gets replaced. I can't be full-time . . . Now, can we order?"

This look was even more severe; if the hash browns had been there I'd have crawled under them. It was the last look I got from her. For the remainder of our stay she dealt only with Spleen. He didn't seem to mind. He struck me as the kind of guy who could allow a great deal to go by and not miss any of it. He let me pay the check – to a cook who stood over the cash register looking like it wouldn't bother him much if he did have to spank me with his waffle iron – and left a three-dollar tip.

It was dark by the time we got out of there. Spleen had me drop him off in the alley next to Lafly's store. He looked around on the ground until he found the remains of a shattered beer bottle, which he began throwing, one piece at a time, at a second story window directly above the store. Nothing happened until the third hit, when a light switched on. Spleen waited a few moments, then threw another piece of glass just as Lafly Senior's head appeared. The glass struck the screen beside Lafly's face.

"All right, goddamnit. You got me to the window, you don't have to throw any more."

"It's me – Spleen."

"I never gave you my telephone number?"

His voice seemed no more tired of life than usual.

"I need to see you, it's important. I have to buy something."

"Come back tomorrow," Lafly said. Then he drawled, "Everything's on sale tomorrow."

"It's got to be tonight. I need it tonight."

"Goddamnit," was all Lafly said before his head disappeared. When the light went off, Spleen went to wait at the shop door.

It was nine o'clock on a week night and the streets were deserted. Spleen looked inward at the friendliness of a sudden desolation. He was on a mission and wished it could attenuate itself for him until he really felt the atavistic ease of stolidity of the man protecting what he has.

He knew the Sneering Brunette would not have expected him to be gone so long. She might even worry, maybe they had come to that. Yet the full of night did not fill him with urgency. Every day he spent with the Sneering Brunette at her hideout, the shades drawn and the music low, had the cast of a long night. That day he woke up there, after noon, staring at the lamp they had left on the night before. The Sneering Brunette laid one of her legs across his, moved her lips to his ear, and murmured, "Spleen." The warmth of her breath and her leg commingled in the strange light of their deflected afternoon. He reached without ardor between her legs and they made love quietly.

The Sneering Brunette, wearing a black slip, cooked eggs while Spleen smoked cigarettes and drank coffee, watching her thighs move about the kitchen. Whenever she glanced at him she must have thought his lust insatiable, but what she couldn't have known was that for Spleen those thighs were passage to a world where thoughts were as elusive as worms that disappear into the earth before you can even get a glimpse of them, and that when she spoke after a long silence, asking him if he was tired yet of having to sneak around like a fugitive in order to see her, her voice came to him out of a black-veiled world beyond the hypnotic dance of her thighs like an occult miracle, something that makes promises both exotic and profane.

He was able to think as the moment materialized before him.

"No, I'm not. My life hasn't been this charged with suspense since the last days on the farm I spent trying not to outwit my father."

"You're an odd man, Spleen."

"It's inadvertent."

She brought their breakfast to the table and they ate while she tried to think of a way to be honest with him and still stay out of trouble. He could tell. He was already able to distinguish from among her different silences and he awaited with pleasure the next foray she would make into the topic that had been designing their new lives for them.

"I was hoping you'd say yes," she said finally.

"So I'd want to leave town?"

"Yes."

"It's been long enough. I still have my legs."

"They're still out there, Spleen. I still have friends."

"What does that mean?"

"Deke's still looking for me. And somebody else, too."

"Who?"

"I think you know."

"Are you sure?"

"Who else could it be? Spleen, I know people at unemployment. They said somebody called there trying to get my address. They asked about you."

She had stopped eating. The remaining egg on her plate was vehemently indifferent. Spleen pondered the post-breakfast landscape; he studied the tenacity of the yolk on the tines of her fork which slumped forlorn and sideways on her plate.

"We'll have to give it some thought," he said.

"We've *been* giving it some thought," she countered, refusing to suppress all of her exasperation. "What *do* you think about, Spleen? Do you think about me?" Her words were now sidling up to him like a kitten. "Why don't you ever ask me about myself? Don't you want to know me?"

Spleen stopped chewing the last of his toast, much of which was balled up in his cheek, and looked straight into her eyes. He held them a few seconds, then resumed chewing.

"Is that a bad question?"

Spleen pointed to his face.

"Wait till you're done chewing, right?"

Spleen nodded.

He chewed slowly.

The Sneering Brunette sensed that he was stalling.

"Christ, Spleen, forget it. I didn't mean to stun you with a personal question. I don't even know what I'm thinking of. I have no idea who the fuck you even are and I'm thinking I want to run away with you. It's fucking ridiculous. I'm too goddamn romantic."

Spleen swallowed.

"So, tell me about yourself."

"I'll tell you one thing about myself, you smug bastard. I'm a lot more curious about you than you are about me."

"What do you want to know?"

"For one thing, what are you doing? I don't mean to criticize, but what are you up to? You don't do anything.

You don't have a job and don't seem to be looking for one. You read a little now and then. You spend time with me, but never say anything . . ."

"That's not true – we talk."

"Sure, but it's only day-to-day stuff. You have no plan or anything. You never talk about the future. What are you doing?"

Spleen got up to clear the table. More stalling. He'd been duped into thinking he'd fallen into a life that would never change, a free zone that required no past and belonged to no future. Or he'd been duped into not thinking at all, taken in by the invisibility of the pressures that persuade circumstances out of the shallow ditches they thrive in. He and the Sneering Brunette never spoke about love, and so he tried not to think about it, but just the night before she had cooked Cornish game hens for him, a gesture as unfamiliar to him as love offered free of tentacles, and so a gesture easily mistaken for love.

"Nobody's ever cooked gamish corn hens for me before," he had said.

"I've never cooked them for anyone before."

"I don't believe it."

"You like them?"

She had pulled her chair up next to his and eaten with a hand on his thigh. With a Cornish game hen leg in his hand, he had put his arm around her, pulled her close, and smeared sauce on her cheek with his lips.

"I love it. It's so succulent I feel like I'm eating an infant."

"You always know what to say, don't you?" she'd said.

"You don't know what to say, do you, Spleen?" she

said now. "Well, you're done cleaning the table – you want to maybe make the bed now? Clean the bathtub?"

Spleen sat down again at the table. He looked in her eyes again. They looked different now.

"You're really mad, aren't you?"

"No, Spleen, I'm not mad. I'm frustrated. I don't know anything. I'm a fucked-up woman – obviously. I spent ten years with a homicidal maniac. Now I've fallen in love with you – sorry to finally say it – and I don't know what I expect; I don't know if I'm just grateful you've stayed with me this long or grateful you overlook my past, but – "

"You're not grateful."

The Sneering Brunette stood abruptly, running her fingers through her hair. Spleen looked at her body in her black slip, looked at the ease of her dishevelment, recognized the sort of damp odorless intimacy she was suggesting, and he wanted to find a way to equate for her his acquiescence with the moments she refused to disguise her failures.

"I need a cigarette," she said.

She left to retrieve the cigarettes from the bedroom. When she returned Spleen was relieved that she had not changed out of her slip. He thought to himself that he would always believe what a woman said to him in the afternoon if she was dressed that way. She sat down again, lit a cigarette, and exhaled without anger.

"All right. I'm not grateful. Thanks. That was a nice thing to say. You're a nice man. And you're mysterious. It keeps me interested and ten miles away."

"That was a good meal last night. I thought maybe I might love you, too."

Now Spleen caught himself looking for gratitude. All he saw was the cigarette that fell sarcastic from her lips. He picked it off the table and put it in his mouth.

"You almost said something nice there, Spleen. You almost did it."

Spleen knew immediately that a line had been crossed making desperation possible and disaster inevitable. She would never love him again without hatred, and she would never forgive herself for either. Spleen had suddenly been deprived of the responsibility for their equilibrium. With or without his help she would arrange the components of their chaos into an increasingly sloppy and preposterous enactment of love, enabling the distortions of passion to remain beyond their mutual capacities to adjust to them. They would evolve immunities it would take years to recognize with horror. He knew with absolute certainty that the only sensible thing to do would be to leave immediately and never see her again, and as soon as he saw himself knowing that he embraced her exuberantly with the remaining strength of his defeated being. He wondered if love was nothing more than the decision to say yes, I will be unhappy with you; if it was what comes after you are banished from your furtive eden, when you look back and decide yes, that was a good enough memory to reward with the resolve to see the dissipation through to the end. Spleen looked at the sneering lip of the Sneering Brunette and, for the first time since meeting her, spoke despite looking deep inside himself for the right words and finding that they weren't there.

"I love you," Spleen said. "I really do."

They made love on the kitchen floor, and the Sneering

Brunette misunderstood with delight Spleen's request that she not remove her slip.

"Let me tell you something," Spleen said afterwards as they lay on the floor, their sore bodies relieved not to be moving. "My brother is supporting me because he could be me. He's my twin, and in many ways we really are almost the same. Somehow he became successful, but he could easily have gone the same way I did. You could look at it as an experiment. He's allowed himself to do things he never really decided to do, made decisions without taking things into consideration that he didn't have enough information to take into consideration. If you want to know what I'm doing, that's it: I'm taking things into consideration."

"But for how long? It could go on forever."

"And what if it did?"

The Sneering Brunette paused to consider.

"But it can't," she decided. "Eventually you'll die."

"That's what I mean."

"But isn't there anything you want?"

"*You* ask me that?"

"To do. Anything you want to do."

"Yes, but all my mentors are dead. They lived in different worlds. I want to be a prophet. I want to see how to do what I want in the future."

"Now you lost me."

"What about you? What do you want now that you're retired from the County?"

"I want to stop being fucked up."

Spleen rolled toward her.

"You're not fucked up."

"Did you forget what Barlow told you?"

"You made mistakes. You wouldn't make them now."

Spleen stood and began dressing.

"What are you doing?"

"I'm going to go buy a gun."

"A gun?" Lafly pushed the door shut behind Spleen. "At least you had the sense not to scream about that in the alley. What the hell do you want a gun for? To kill yourself? Rob a liquor store? What the hell do you need a gun for?"

"Protection."

Lafly made his face wider and began speaking without stops.

"Against what for Christ's sake you can't protect yourself against anything, you going to shoot the goddamn IRS, get away from the windows, here follow me."

Lafly led Spleen to where he'd never been – "Watch yourself you don't knock over any of these goddamn antiques" – down the narrow path past the slot machine, past cases filled with pocketknives, hat pins, compasses, pens bearing the logos of defunct gas stations, zippos, medallions, rosary beads, past lamps with and without lampshades, past golf clubs, felt hats, alarm clocks, music boxes, globes, books, magnifying glasses, photographs, maps, everything piled without pretense on top of old desks and crates filled with plates and wax gargoyle figurines and *National Geographics* and fishing lures and oil paints, and through the Art Deco swinging tavern door Lafly said was worth a thousand dollars, under the Art Deco chandelier Lafly said was worth two thousand dollars, into the inner sanctum where Lafly himself usually sat or stood hitching up his pants announcing that everything was on sale that

day, and farther still, past the bathroom, to a door Lafly unlocked that opened on stairs that led to a basement Lafly
said no one knew about, not even his own goddamn
brother, and which if Spleen ever opened his mouth about
could get Lafly in a great deal of trouble and perhaps earn
Spleen a belly wound from one of the guns Lafly kept down
there.

"Watch your step," Lafly told him as they started
down. He used a weak flashlight to locate the fuzzy outlines
of each step.

"There's no light switch," Lafly said when he reached
the basement floor. "You'll have to wait here . . . keeps peo
ple from nosing around."

Spleen thought about that, his hand resting against the
wall to assure himself that the darkness could be contained.

"Who would even try?" he called out finally.

A fuzzy ball of light looped back toward Spleen.

"Those goddamn IRS boys'll try anything. You'll catch
them rooting around your goddamn toilet if you're not
careful, going through your goddamn turds."

The light made its way to the back wall, having followed a tortuous pattern that took it from one wall of the
basement to the other, forming several ephemeral geometric
shapes as it went, often losing itself behind Lafly or whatever else was lurking in the dark.

Spleen expected a light to come on and expose a
maze of some kind of contraband, maybe an underground
outdoor shop, with racks of guns everywhere, and moose-
heads, but what he got was a small desk lamp by which he
could barely make out the path between literally dozens of
locked wood cabinets, most of which had nothing on top of
them, though in the very center of the room there was a

ten-foot headless statue of a mermaid, apparently bronze.

Seeing that he had stopped to appraise it, Lafly called to him, "That's the real one. The one at San Lupe de Vidalgo's a fake. You can guess yourself how much it's worth."

Spleen finally met up with Lafly at the back wall, which turned out to be a single, massive cabinet that went from wall to wall and rose nearly to the ceiling. Up against it was a marble table with wrought iron legs comprised of a series of leaping dogs, probably greyhounds. The lamp was on the table between a violin and a stuffed pigeon. The pigeon had an envelope crammed into its beak.

Lafly patted the table.

"Once sat in a nook in the Versailles Palace. You've heard of that, haven't you?"

"And the violin's a Stradivarius, right?"

"No, it's not. It was made by a man named Emilio Vittorini. Made especially for Paganini. Worth tens of thousands, got to be."

"And the pigeon?"

"That's a homing pigeon. Carrier pigeon. Now extinct."

"Once used by Marco Polo to send a letter home."

"If you want to be a smart ass you can – "

"I'm sorry . . . What's in all these cabinets?"

"Don't ask any questions. This one's the gun cabinet." Lafly indicated the cabinet that took up the back wall. "That's all you need to know. Think of the rest as empty."

"Just tell me one. If you were worried about me opening my mouth you wouldn't have shown me this much. Unless you think the IRS will use truth serum on me, but even then – "

"All right. Which one?"

Spleen looked the cabinets over until he spotted a walnut cabinet in the shape of a female torso.

"That one, the voluptuous one."

"Rhino horn."

"You've got to be kidding."

"No."

"And that's really a carrier pigeon?"

The pigeon was uniformly gray and seemed no larger than the average La Crosse pigeon.

"Go ahead and read the letter."

Spleen plucked the envelope out of the beak and removed the letter.

"I don't read German."

The letterhead was a cathedral and the address underneath was Seven Friedrichstrasse, Trier.

"It's a love letter," Lafly said. "You can read the date, can't you? 1818, the year Karl Marx was born – in Trier. The letter was written by his uncle to his aunt, but not the right one, get it . . . you know the story, German hijinks. They were discovered but they keep things like that quiet over there."

Spleen put the letter back in the envelope and returned it to the pigeon's beak.

"I won't ask if it's the same pigeon."

"What do you need the gun for?"

"I told you – protection."

"I remember. Protection from what?"

"It's a long story. The fact of the matter is I need a gun."

Lafly backed himself up to a cabinet that was about three feet high, rested his palms on it, and lifted himself to sit.

"Nothing's on sale tonight," he drawled. "I've got a bazooka, but that's out of your range. I've got hand grenades, but you didn't say you wanted a hand grenade – besides, innocent people get hurt. I've got deer rifles, but you aren't going deer-hunting. I've got all kinds of pistols, but I don't know what you're going to use them for. Come to think of it, I've even got crossbows, but you'd have to practice to be worth a shit at it, and if you need a gun tonight you haven't got time to practice . . . No, Spleen, I won't be able to help you unless what you're looking for is an old Ivers-Johnson .22 pistol that I could give you for free if I knew why you wanted it – the whole story."

"What's an Ivers-Johnson .22 pistol?"

Lafly laughed.

"It's a gun. You wanted a goddamn gun, it's a gun."

"I can have it if I tell you why I want it?"

"You can have it free. It isn't worth five bucks. If the IRS boys found it they'd call it an antique and claim it was worth five hundred. I don't need the goddamn gun. But I'm not going to let you have it unless I know what you plan to do with it. If you kill somebody with it I want it to be self-defense . . ."

"You remember that time I was upstairs we were talking about Jimmy's leap and that brunette came up to me?" Spleen began, and proceeded to tell Lafly all about Deke Dobson and the fugitive Richie Buck, and about Frank Barlow and the Fag With No Eyebrows and Billy Verité. The only one he'd seen lately was the Sneering Brunette, who still felt threatened and was hiding out. As far as he knew, if there ever really was a threat it had passed by now.

"But you still want to buy a gun?"

"She says they're still trying to find her. They being

Dobson and Buck. She wants to leave town. I don't – not yet. The gun is a compromise."

"What if you need the gun?"

Spleen shrugged.

"I'll tell you what if you need the gun. If you need the gun it won't help you a goddamn bit and I'll tell you why. If somebody wants to break your legs for you or kill you or whatever he wants to do with you he's not going to announce it to you so you can get your gun ready first. He's not going to knock on your front door and when you ask who it is say I'm the guy who's going to break your legs. What he is going to do is catch you by surprise – get the drop on you – and incapacitate you immediately. No goddamn gun is going to save you. So you want the gun, listen to a piece of advice. There's a movie called *Charley Varrick*. Have you seen the movie?"

"No."

"Well, you're not going to see it, you're going to tell me you'll see it so I'll give you the gun, so I'm not going to give you the gun until I tell you the story. I don't want you running around out there with my gun in your hand and your head up your ass. Walter Matthau plays a bank robber named Charley Varrick. Varrick robs a bank, a little bank in New Mexico, small town, small bank, Varrick figures to pick up a few grand. Only it turns out the bank is a drop for the mafia. Varrick and one of his partners – the other two get dead – make off with three-quarters of a million dollars. Varrick's partner, young kid, war vet or some goddamn thing, gets all excited, he's never seen that much money in his whole life, but he sees Walter Matthau isn't all that happy to be rich. Well that's because Varrick's been around, he knows you don't get that kind of money out of some goddamn hick bank unless something's very wrong, he knows they're in big trouble now, they aren't just going to have the feds after them, the mafia'll hunt them down and kill them without asking questions. The kid asks how long before they can spend the money and Varrick tells the kid at least three or four years. The kid doesn't understand that, he sees all that money and thinks they can just run and keep running, and Varrick knows that even if the kid agrees to wait he can't keep his mouth shut that long, there's no way to keep him from spending the money anyway, so Varrick writes the kid off right away. He's a hothead, he won't listen. Nothing can save him. And he knows he can't give the money back – they'll kill him anyway, you don't make the mafia look bad and live to tell about it, they have to set an example. You know how those guys are. He can't run, they'll find him sooner or later, probably sooner, a few days. So you see, Varrick's got the most powerful crime organization in the world after him, he can't return the money, he can't run, what the hell can he do? I'll tell you what he does, the only thing he can do, he goes on the attack. No, he doesn't go off half-cocked and start shooting everybody he sees who looks like a wop, they don't even look Italian, hell, some of them these days aren't Italian. The guy they send after Varrick is Joe Don Baker – he's not Italian. Mean, though, big methodical killer, sadistic, you know the type, easygoing, slit his own mother's throat . . . What Varrick does is make like he's planning to flee the country, just what they'd expect him to do, but he leaves a trail, see, because the problem with the enemy is he can't see it. Only thing he can do is meet the enemy head on, but he's got to flush him out first. The enemy's off guard, they aren't expecting Varrick to come after them, he's got their money, he's going to run. That's the one advantage he has, surprise. He leaves a trail and he finds out the enemy is Joe Don Baker when Joe Don Baker finds his trailer and tortures the kid to death, ugly scene, poor goddamn kid, but Varrick isn't there, he's outside hiding in the weeds, hell there was nothing he could do for the kid. Now Varrick finds out who the mob front man is, the guy in charge of laundering the money, keeping the IRS boys off the trail, see, the guy who put the money in that bank in the first place, Varrick calls him and says I want to give you your money back, I'll meet you but you have to come alone, keep that goddamn goon away from me or you don't get your money back. Well, he's not stupid, he knows Joe Don Baker will be hiding somewhere no matter what he says, so he sets it up that way, I'm not going to go into it, but when he meets the guy he knows Joe Don Baker is watching. What he does is greet the front man like the two of them had a deal all along, like they were splitting the money, the robbery was all arranged, Varrick keeps yelling 'We did it, we did it,' jumping up and down and hollering, slapping him on the back and hugging him, so Joe Don Baker thinks the front man's a traitor, he's hiding in a junk lot in his car and sees this and goes after the other guy, kills him, then goes after Varrick, who makes like he's trying to get away in his airplane, fakes a wreck, tells Joe Don Baker where the money is, in the trunk of that goddamn car over there, and Joe Don Baker falls for it, opens the trunk and Varrick's got it rigged with dynamite, see, blows him up, makes it look like he got blown up, too, by throwing his jumpsuit with his name on it in there, throws in a few bills to make it look good, like the money's all gone, too, and Varrick drives away with the money and nobody after him, see, because he met his goddamn enemy head on, he didn't run away until they caught him or keep a gun in his pants waiting for them to ask if he wanted to shoot them, see?"

Lafly slid off the cabinet, reaching into his pocket for his keys at the same time. There were fewer than ten keys on a silver ring the size of a bracelet. Spleen wondered if all the cabinets had the same lock.

"Look someplace else," Lafly said.

He was crouching to unlock the cabinet he'd been sitting on. Spleen stared at the big cabinet, refusing to imagine what firepower was nestled within.

"All right, you can turn around."

Lafly handed Spleen a pistol. The metal was the color of lead. The butt was made of wood. The barrel was long and thin and much less ominous than Spleen would have supposed. He hefted the gun, waiting to feel happy, and then he remembered the next thing to do was point it at something. He aimed it at the stuffed carrier pigeon, aligned the small fin at the end of the barrel with the canaliculus atop the hammer, and pulled the trigger. A dull click clicked.

6

The reliance of sedentary people upon laws destroys their fortitude and power of resistance.

— Abd-ar-Rahman Abu Zayd ibn
Muhammed ibn Muhammed ibn Khaldun

"La illaha illah Allah. Mohammedan rasulu." Heads turn throughout the brown flat-roofed city spired by minarets, laced with tile, perfumed by gardens, split by broad avenues lined with plane trees. Waists bend, heads hit mats, the spiritual compass needle points south-southwest. It's a very holy city, so holy, they say, even the birds respect prayer time, grounding themselves to keep out of the way of all those prayers being tossed to Mecca – but who would know, everybody tapping their heads on the ground, nobody looking up? Who would know? The kaftaarbaz. The pigeon boys. They would know. At prayer time in Tehran only the kaftaarbaz remain oblivious of God. They have no time; every second of every day must be devoted to their pigeons. The kaftaarbaz, the pigeon boys, alone have their eyes on birds at prayer time. In Tehran the kaftaarbaz constitute a social problem of unimaginable proportions. They're an insoluble problem. No ayatollah, no imported modern psychiatrist, no hypnotist, no Savak, no parental guidance can cure the kaftaarbaz. When a Tehrani boy goes to the pigeons he's gone forever.

Take the little Farsi boy. Call him Mohsen. Perhaps he's a little quieter than the others, but besides that he seems normal. He likes to fly kites, eat plums, listen to *Arabian Nights* stories at bedtime; he's a little confused by and impatient with pomegranates, likes to kick stones, makes fun of girls. One day, he may be ten or eleven, maybe even as old as eighteen, he sees a pigeon in the courtyard and it has a broken wing. Or he inexplicaby becomes fascinated by the activity on a neighbor's roof, the strange absorption of another boy's movements. Or he may be initiated by a kaftaarbaz he happens to befriend somehow. Most often the origins of the disease cannot be traced; but the Persians are a sad and poetic people, so they imagine it happens at night, when the bird and boy are possessed by the same moon; in the blue night the silver bird flies into the silver moon that disappears into the boy's heart. And suddenly Mohsen has a pet pigeon on the roof, suddenly Mohsen is breeding pigeons on the roof. It becomes difficult to get him to meals on time. Before school he cannot be found, for he has risen before the others and is already up on the roof. Mohsen soon quits going to school. Once he makes it to the roof it's impossible to get him down before bedtime without using force, and force will never work, for such is the unnatural affinity the kaftaarbaz has for his birds that he will die if separated from them for long. He cannot eat, his bowels no longer function, his mind begins to waste away, memories drop off like feathers from a diseased bird; he's sunken into a grave lassitude, a hopeless torpor, that none of his previous passions – no sweets, for instance – nor any kind of medical attention nor force can alleviate. If he is not soon back with his birds he will die. Relatives of Mohsen will meet acquaintances at shops and say with an acquiescence common to peoples along the tragic latitudes of life, "Our Mohsen has gone to the birds." Gone to the birds. Even Mohsen's parents will say it eventually. He will be placed in the same category as the lunatic uncle locked away in an asylum who is taken on a disastrous outing once a year – only Mohsen will cause less trouble. They will have to take him his food, clean up after him, bathe him now and then, and that's all. As long as he is left with his birds he will be happy.

The phenomenon of the kaftaarbaz cannot be explained. It goes beyond the affair Marlon Brando has with his pigeons in *On the Waterfront*. For Marlon the pigeons are only an amusing diversion, no different really from a boy's habit of playing stickball, or mastering the yo-yo, or walking the railroad tracks. Spleen never kept pigeons, but he paid attention to them, and perhaps he loved them – yet they never threatened to become an obsession. Spleen singled out the pigeon because it's the quintessential urban bird, the bird of Roman omen; he loved the bird (if he did) for an idea, and as long as he could carry the idea around with him he didn't need the pigeon. So it must be assumed that with the kaftaarbaz it's an entirely different matter, having nothing to do with the brain; nor even the emotions – Spleen's idea having been necessitated by an emotional reaction. It's probably not even worth mentioning that it's hardly a matter of mastery, either. The kaftaarbaz train their pigeons to come and not go far, to hop about as directed, sometimes to fight the birds of other kaftaarbaz, but nothing astonishing enough to explain the utter captivation of the boy by the bird. Even if they could resurrect the carrier pigeon it would not be enough to explain the way these birds capture the Tehrani boy's soul. Too many other animals perform better tricks. And it *is* a matter of the soul (or call it spirit), for the pigeons steal the boy's very life; they become as essential for sustenance as the very air he breathes. I know of no phenomenon quite like it. The closest I can think of is the case of the old men in Hong Kong who take their budgies or finches or parakeets for walks, carrying the beautiful bamboo cages to parks and waterfronts. Taking the birds for air. That, too, is an odd habit, and probably as well a matter of spirit – bird and man share a majestic detachment; if there is indeed a *reason* for the old man to take his bird for a walk, it *must* be spiritual. Which suggests that perhaps a sort of bird/man nexus/continuum exists, the Farsi boys being the most extreme example of man being connected to bird. It would be useless to try to explain why the locus of such excrescence happens to be one place rather than another; the fact of the matter is that it *could* well be no more than an extraordinary manifestation of a condition essentially human. We know of many people who wish they were birds, or at least envy them their flight. The cabdriver/owner Arbogast told me that his parents used to think he was "slow" because as a kid he used to spend hours in his room staring at the ceiling, seeing at first stars, then rising in flight and seeing the Earth below. And, of course, now man does fly (rendering even the idea of the carrier pigeon extinct), which would never have been possible without an uncommon degree of identification between man-spirit and bird-spirit.

Where there is the possibility of a spirit-draining love, there is also the possibility of a baffling ambivalence. Richie Buck, the man who ate the head of a pigeon called Nadine, lived in a tent on the Island, and when he was not engaged in his nefarious human entanglements in town, he was spending his time befriending the birds indigenous to the Island forest. It is inconceivable that the spirit of man is not yielding its most sublime aspect when in comportment with the birds, yet for the svelte and incommunicative bird-spirit within Buck to exist beside the demonstrably brute darkness of his soul is a monstrous proposition, mere consideration of which can be as harrowing as the unwavering examination of pure evil. With a sated mallard on his lap, its head shoved in slumber under its wing, and a blue jay hopping from one of his shoulders to the other, Buck contemplated the Spleen dilemma with a feathery equanimity that belied on his part the inability to look back satisfied on several jobs well done as long as one remained. Buck was a far different thinker from Deke Dobson. There were leaves everywhere, but for each leaf there were holes that let in leaves of sunlight. He held his arm out straight. The sun leapt from his shoulder to his hand, five leaves of sun. He snapped his fingers. The blue jay leaped from leaf to leaf down to his hand. Buck snatched the blue jay's feet and leaped to his own, sending the duck bounding away; it awoke as if from an ambiguous dream and marched back to squawk at Buck's shins. Buck held the struggling blue jay upside down, letting it peck at his fingers. "Speak up, boy," Buck said, but the blue jay continued to fight silently. "Pathetic fuck," Buck called it, wondering briefly whether or not he should stomp on its skull and then cook it. The blue jay finally gave up, hanging limp from Buck's fingers, panting in rapid spurts. Satisfied for reasons he ignored for their murk, Buck wound up and pitched the bird into the sky with much of his might, shouting, "Go tell Spleen his days are numbered!" The blue jay hit a low branch of a birch tree and plummeted back to the ground, then lurched to its feet and ran into a takeoff without looking back.

Buck walked through the forest to the riverslough, the duck following behind, contented *aks* escaping from it now and then. At the slough they stood side by side, contemplating the reflections of the trees opposite, resistant and darker on the flowing water. You can't just break a man's legs and hope to get away with it. No – you had to kill him. But who was this Spleen? Who was Spleen to a fugitive like Richie Buck? Was he in his arbitrary role of imminent victim proof to Buck of the fragility of man's existence? Could an inversion of sorts have taken place, so that murdering Spleen was Buck's revenge against the architects of his own predicament? If Buck was not a man to reflect deeply, and if Spleen meant nothing to him as a specific being, does it follow that while Spleen was off somewhere in the city acting suspicious of every manifestation of meaning he encountered that Buck as his executioner would be settling the question for him? Buck could not see a specific Spleen; he could only see an Everyman Spleen, a Spleen representative of all men. And as any man would, Spleen represented the potential to be hated – but Buck would have to see him first (then hatred would be inevitable). Until then he contemplated Spleen's murder without enmity. Spleen as Spleen meant nothing. Spleen as Everyman meant nothing. Spleen must die.

Who was Spleen? Someone Buck had to find before he could kill him. Someone Detective Stratton suspected of a murder he had not committed. Buck stood beside his friend the duck, looking at the trees across the slough that did not escape with the current. Buck and the duck were happy. It was a warm summer morn and they did not know that the bucolic quiet was an absence of blue herons. Buck looked down at the duck and said, "I'll find Stratton. He'll lead me to Spleen."

Stratton, so far unfollowed, covered the ground from his car to the front door of the house in unconsciously jaunty steps. He rapped merrily on the door. The woman who answered had blonde hair, sunken cheeks, a stale redness rimming her eyes, dark pouches under them, and wrinkles fanning out from their corners. She looked like she was immersed in a withering anemia of grief. "Come in, Detective Stratton," she said. That meant she knew him. Could it be her? he wondered. She wore a long sheer nightgown that if it were her would have met the resistance of more and curvaceous flesh. He tried to remember if she had a sister. He didn't think so. She led him into the kitchen where the black undercover cop sat reading a newspaper and drinking coffee.

"Hey, buddy," the black undercover cop said when he saw Stratton. "Had breakfast yet?"

"Nope."

"Honey, fry up some eggs for Detective Stratton."

"Yes, love," the woman said blandly.

Stratton took another good look at her face. It was her all right. What a prize she turned out to be, he thought.

"Any news?" he asked the black undercover cop.

"Not about Spleen. You?"

"No. The son of a bitch either left town or he's hiding."

"What about from – honey, hurry up on those eggs and get out of here so we can talk."

"Yes, love."

"My friend, Billy Verité, wouldn't know what to do outside this town. He's got to be hiding somewhere."

"Well, I suppose as long as he's hiding we've really got nothing to worry about."

"Any contact with Mr. X?"

"None."

"Think he's still around?"

"No bodies have turned up."

The black undercover cop jerked his head to indicate the stiffened form of the woman at the stove.

"Nobody has turned up? To identify him?"

"That's what I meant. Nobody's turned up to identify him."

They maintained a strained silence until the woman set a plate with two eggs and two slices of toast in front of Stratton. As she tried to move off, the black undercover cop nabbed one of her wrists. Stratton took little note of the fear she couldn't conceal by smiling and repeating, "Yes, love?"

"You remembered he likes his eggs over easy?"

The smile went rigid on her face and her eyes became a little wider.

"You like your eggs over easy, partner?"

"Sure do," Stratton said, putting a forkful onto his toast.

"See? Then you did the right thing, honey. Now go up-stairs for a bit."

He released her wrist and she went away.

"No bodies have turned up," the black undercover cop said, "but I know of one I haven't seen for a long time."

Stratton nodded and smiled. "Me too," he said through a mouth full of eggs and toast.

"But I do have a surprise for you. No word on Spleen, like I said. But it seems he has a brother, an identical twin whom we'll call Spleen Two. He works for the newspaper. He should be a pretty easy man to find, and I suspect he'll know where we can locate his brother."

Stratton could not believe what he was hearing, or that if he was hearing what he thought he was hearing he hadn't heard it the minute he walked into the kitchen. He decided to test the waters.

"What?"

"You heard right."

"Spleen has an identical twin?"

"That's right."

"Another Spleen? Spleen Two? You waited? Let's haul his ass in for questioning. Right now."

Stratton stood with the abrupt economy of an angry man. The black undercover cop reached for the piece of toast on Stratton's plate.

"Why do people always assume there's a one-to-one correspondence between eggs and toast? Oh, there's an-other surprise, something we'd like to ask you. We'd like you to be best man at our wedding."

"What are you talking about? Let's go get that son of a bitch."

"Sit down, partner."

Stratton remained standing, his shoulders twitching.

"Sit down? This is our first lead in weeks and you want me to sit down?"

"About the wedding. Yes or no? We'll need an answer soon."

"The wedding? Fuck the goddamn wedding and let's go grill that bastard."

"Fuck the wedding? Did I hear you say fuck the wedding?"

Stratton slapped his forehead.

"You're always doing this. You can't keep your mind on one thing anymore. We've got a case to solve here."

"I hope I didn't hear you say fuck the wedding."

"Christ. What do I have to – look, all right, I'll be your best man. Now what about this Spleen Two, can we go now or what?"

"I can't believe you said fuck the wedding."

"Damn it, I'm sorry I said fuck the wedding. Now can we go?"

"This wedding is the most important event in my life and you tell me to fuck it."

"I'm sorry. I said I was sorry. I'm very sorry. I'll be your best man. Can we go and get this son of a bitch now?"

"Promise me you won't say fuck the wedding again."

"I promise."

"Promise what?"

"I promise I won't fucking say fuck the goddamn wedding again."

"The goddamn wedding?"

"Will you stop?"

"The goddamn wedding?"

"I never gave marriage any thought," Spleen said, "but I suppose I have nothing against it."

The Sneering Brunette ran her hand over the bristles on Spleen's head.

"You think I'm being foolish, don't you?"

Spleen wished he could think she was being foolish. He wished he knew enough or had the assurance of character to override his own ignorance, that he could slap her arm aside and wear a gray fedora, leap to his feet and pace the floor before her, his cigarette dropping ashes on her feet as he gestured angrily, telling her yes she was a fool and this is how things were going to be; or that he could drop to his knees before her and, his hair black and brilliantined, elongate his thin mustache seductively, wipe a tear from her eye while lighting two cigarettes in his mouth, offer her one and say no you aren't a fool, it is I who have been a fool, there is a beach in a town called Progreso, north of Mérida, we shall go there you and I, mi amor, mi corazon, we will go today if you will still have me; but he had bristles on his head and her hand was soft and he didn't know, he didn't know if she was being foolish, he didn't know how to answer or how to act, for he was a man who sought to value integrity and could only manage the integrity of an inaction based on a lack of conviction – he had only this resolute uncertainty to abide by, which he did with ease and without pride, knowing with an increasingly tense resignation that the only way to ensure failure was by failing to act. The Sneering Brunette was the force of time and movement, and he was an insignificant shape of stillness without the capacity for resistance or transcendence.

"So you think I'm being foolish, then. Or is it that you think I'm trying to trick you into leaving with me?"

"No," Spleen said without enthusiasm.

"No what?"

"I don't know if you're being foolish."

Spleen knew immediately that he'd said the wrong thing. Her hand froze on top of his head and her eyes went vague, looking out the window or at the reflection of the dismal amber room the night turned back at her.

Spleen looked past her head at the cheap panelling and the oil painting of a weak sun setting over pines behind a northern lake. When his eyes settled on the painting, the two of them could have been looking at the same thing, the Sneering Brunette's version darkened by the real night that heaved against the motel room, sheltering the phantasms she could not persuade Spleen to recognize. And if Billy Verité was out there, crouched behind a bush, paralyzed by uncertainty – could she see him? If Billy was out there – wouldn't she see only the reflection? If Billy was out there, bored by the mute and sluggish puppet show inside, afraid to move, his wandering eyes seduced into the verisimilitude of a mediocre painting, then that would make three. Three of them in three different ways for three different reasons, each without considering the grim possibilities vis-à-vis meaning, for instance that the moments of consuming blandness between the harassments of furious activity are inferior to the quality of the escape offered by oil paints applied by habits enabled only by an abject admission of defeat on the part of the human spirit, each of the three fading, becoming invisible, attracted to a peace removed once from its origins by election to archetypal status, once again by its conception in the mind of the perpetrator, again by his son who said well, if nobody else wants it, by the son's wife who offered it up at a garage sale, once more by the boy who picked junk for his antique dealer father and who offered fifty cents for it, once again by his father who reluctantly hung it in his shop and was soon so sick of it he said to the new owner of an old motel no deal on the lamps unless you take this goddamn picture off my hands too, and removed once again by said motel owner who asked really? for free?, and hung it in one of his dismal amber rooms for it to be removed again and again by his guests whose un-dramatic, unspecialized, insoluble or unconquerable or self-imposed *and* quixotic troubles or aspirations or uneasi-nesses were not put to rest by the television and so turned to a vision of peace that came free with the room and could instill in them an imperceptible admiration for the en-durance of stagnation and an unconscious desire to reside in that place where the sun never sets and there is no tem-perature and the trees are ever green, and removed three more times then, by Spleen, who would see in the painting the ceaseless white escapings of his thoughts, by the Sneering Brunette, who would see a less benign Spleen, and by Billy Verité, who would see in it the dignity of his profes-sion, which he measured by the successful forestalling of his impatience. Billy Verité's foot was asleep, but he would not allow himself to move until the Sneering Brunette was no longer staring his way.

The Sneering Brunette brought her hand back to her lap, turned her gaze involuntarily from the window to the painting, and sighed with the agitation of one who can't manage to be bored.

"You can't even say I'm not being foolish. You have to say you don't know."

"How about if I say I don't think it matters? One way or the other."

He put his hand on her forearm, but she shook it off.

She would be the gray fedora type.

She stood to get a cigarette.

Billy Verité would tell you that one way to get to know people would be to spy on them; you'd find them infinitely fascinating. After a while you get pretty good at figuring out what's going on in a room even if you can't hear what the people are saying. What had Spleen said before to bring everything to a halt? Easy: he told her if you want to keep it fine, but you're not going to tie me down. Now look at her, standing in her black slip, one hand on her belly – see? – the other sticking a cigarette in her face (that's real good for the kid), turned away from Spleen, who just tried to console her: I'll pay for it, either way, but nothing is sufficient for her, nothing short of marriage, the noose.

Spleen had his hands on her shoulders; he kissed her neck.

"I know you don't believe me. You think I'm paranoid, but someone had been there. I could tell somebody had gone through my things."

Spleen dropped his arms to his sides and turned from her.

Now look at her, suddenly all friendly, sitting on his lap, thinking if she fucks him he'll change his mind. As if he's going to fall for that. Look at his face: he knows what she's up to and it disgusts him.

"*I* don't even know what I think," Spleen said, "how could *you* possibly know?"

"Is that an answer? Christ – now you don't even want to fuck me?"

"You brought it up, not me. You said *you* don't want to. I didn't say a word about it. It's . . ."

"What? It's what?"

"Nothing."

"Don't start doing that. What were you going to say?"

"I – I was going to say it's getting difficult even to know how to be polite."

Just what you'd expect next – tears. You aren't going to fall for that one, are you, Spleen? No. And look: as if by magic the tears are gone. You can take it from me, Billy Verité, women can turn them on and off like a goddamn faucet. Typical female. What's next? Anger?

"For one thing, what the fuck difference does it make who it was?"

"Please listen: all I'm saying is that I wonder why they didn't stick around to wait for you, that's all. I believe you – really; I just don't get their methods."

Spleen sat on the bed beside her, took the cigarette out of her hand, and made use of it.

"I believe you," he said again.

He'd like to slap her one, but he's got too much class for that. There, the gun. The gun? Why would Spleen have a gun in his hand? Ah, I see it – she's being melodramatic, tears, hysterics, everything, so now he's being melodramatic, too, just to show her what a fool she's being. He's saying here's the gun, go ahead, shoot me. Want me to stop seeing other women? This is the only way, baby – you're going to have to plug me. Can't do it, can you? Now who's the one without guts?

"Maybe you're right, Spleen, but that doesn't give me

any less reason to be scared. Maybe I expected too much from you . . . Come here, make love to me . . ."

Spleen lay down next to her and looked into her eyes. She draped a leg around his waist and looked at his neck and he knew they were about to enact a lie. He pressed his lips to her forehead – she was thinking, too. Spleen ran his hand from her thigh up to her waist, under her slip. He wondered if she was telling him the same thing he was telling her. He thought of the Ivers-Johnson .22 pistol under the pillow and shivered with embarrassment. Why had he thought buying a gun for her would make her happy? His penis was erect and she touched him and he knew she was wet, though he kept his hand on her waist, and he knew that she was still thinking too, and it was as if they had started standing back to back, each then running as fast as they could in opposite directions with no other thought in their minds but how nice it would be when they saw each other again. He finally touched her between her legs and she gasped as if she were not thinking, and the whole Spleen-edifice of Spleen-thought crumbled, and Spleen knew that all he had to do was tell her I don't believe you or I don't believe this, and then the new Spleen-bastion of Spleen-thought crumbled and he knew that he did believe her, that the threat was real, and that the truth was he was afraid. She rolled on top of him, found his penis without using her hands, and made it disappear.

Like a black widow spider . . . Watch her hand, Spleen, watch her hand sliding up toward the pillow – grab her wrist! I knew you wouldn't fall for that, Spleen. Oldest trick in the book, like those hookers in Vietnam with razor blades in their cunts, or the ones that get you up into their rooms and the guy's there with a sap and next thing you know you wake up in the morning and don't know where you are and all your money's gone, even your shoes – That's it, Spleen, hold her arms behind her – Jesus, look at her move . . .

Panting, wanting Spleen to hold her wrists with one hand and feel her breasts with the other; her eyes closed, wanting to feel helpless and to confuse her desires, to justify the inadequacy of her contentedness, even her potential to please herself, by struggling against the restraint she demanded, despising the tension she loved, the tension a hammock on which her only pleasure lay bruised and hungover, empty from vomiting, dialing a telephone, marvelously spent, attenuated and unafraid. Even the sounds that came out of her were restrained, as if another Spleen were behind her with his arm against her throat. She struggled to free her wrists until Spleen let go and she cried, "No!" and Spleen held them again, and she struggled even more fiercely, and Spleen thought that he had run from her, refusing to look back at the gulf they created by fearing it, and the gulf became wider and black, it became the abyss and it was black, and the blackness was soft and he was tired of running, before him a desert as white as his thoughts, and he stopped running and fell back into an illimitable darkness and it held him, and he forgot everything in the black abyss of her embrace, and he knew with the new Spleen-scaffolding of his new Spleen-thought that he was not afraid, had never been afraid, that it was simply that he did not know, and that the world revolved around his not knowing, wondering when he would realize that he could never know, when he would fall into the embracing correspondence between his ignorance and everything concealed from him by his exoteric universe, fall into her black arms which contained a Russian fatalism of space, the absence, the rest, the nothing that alone, for Spleen, would make action possible. Spleen opened his eyes again and saw her face inches from his, her hair falling around his head; her eyes were closed and her body was working with the grave and concise hysteria of a woman in labor. The noises were huskier now, from her sternum, catching in the back of her throat, sent flying with spit at Spleen's face – her ribs moving like an accordion, her hips like a piston – she was growling, the spit was forming foam that drooled down onto Spleen's neck, that which wasn't sent into his hair, onto his face, and she growled and paused for a moment and Spleen felt her vagina grip his penis, strangling him, and her eyes opened and she saw herself through Spleen's eyes and she laughed, a laugh of seductive self-delight, and closed her eyes again and released Spleen's penis so she could move her hips like a piston again, and growl again, and froth and spit and blind Spleen with her hair, and Spleen felt free to go and watch himself stand up, the Sneering Brunette laboring over him, he with one hand binding her wrists, straining forward, pinching her nipples with his other hand, walk out the door, return inside a different Spleen to look around: a black bra on the lampshade, pants on the floor with underwear inside and socks sticking out as if a man had melted there, wine bottles on the desk, glasses everywhere, on the desk empty, beside the bed, the lamp, full, half-full, empty, stockings on the doorknob, a trail of dresses leading to the bed, five dresses leading to the bed – three nights, five dresses? – towels crumpled beside the bed, sheets and blanket on the floor at the foot of the bed, another bra, another, wastebasket knocked over, tissues balled up surrounding it, a single black high-heeled shoe precariously balanced at the corner of the bed, rocking, always falling, miraculously clinging to the bed, rocking faster, and Spleen blowing her hair out of his eyes, looking at her closed eyes, froth slopping onto his mouth, his neck, his chin, looking at her eyes and seeing what they were seeing and knowing it was time to act, to tell her he would give her everything for the bra on the lampshade, and the way her slip fell to the floor like a sigh, and a river of dresses and stockings, the stiletto heels, the lipstick, and most of all the black abyss of her embrace – he would marry her, take her away and marry her with money from his brother, right away, tonight he will go, tonight, the heel hitting the floor as she finally collapsed in acceptance of her pleasure, breaking free of Spleen's grip, scratching her nails into his shoulders, her chest contracting and then expanding one last time, the note coming out clear and loud and laughing, wiping her face on Spleen's hair, Spleen trying to talk, tell her everything, promise her everything, and slapping her palm over his mouth: "Can't you let me enjoy this," lying on Spleen, panting . . .

I guess she doesn't want to hear it, Spleen. Don't forget the gun. I knew it, he was thinking about the gun all along. Better luck next time, little miss femme fatale; maybe the next guy'll be more of a sucker than Spleen, eh? Give her a little slap and say goodbye, Spleen. All right, forget the slap, I know, you got too much class for that. Give the broad her due. She nearly fucked you to death double-o seven, but look who came out on top . . . What's with the shoe?

"I don't know where the other one is," Spleen said, replacing the shoe.

The Sneering Brunette stared at the shoe as if it were some kind of unfamiliar saurian that would soon be leaving.

Spleen wasn't a mind reader. He knew that sometimes a strange tide of emotion comes over a woman after an orgasm. It was more complicated or mysterious or both than what happened with him, with all men, whose range is limited to wanting to sleep or do it again or go to the store for cigarettes and never come back. Women, he knew, could become possessed by spirits even they could not identify. Spleen had seen them weep for an hour afterward, or curse him or something that was simply "out there," or stare eerily like a cat with one paw in another world. So when the Sneering Brunette refused to let him say a word, he didn't mind. She wanted him to leave for a while, she wanted to be alone. He understood. He wanted to go see his brother, anyway. What he had to tell her was so good, would make her so happy, that he was glad she forced him to wait. The business about the gun was strange – why did she want him to take it if she was in danger? – but her fear was an amorphous, or protean creature, and he never really knew whom she was more afraid for; what really was strange was the calm certitude with which she mentioned the gun, so that only when he had shut the motel room door did what he still failed to understand become lodged like a bullet in his brain.

The motel was barely within the city limits, on Mormon Coulee Boulevard, five miles from downtown. Spleen looked forward to the walk, figuring it would take an hour and a half to reach the newspaper, where his brother would still be working. He walked down the gravel drive toward the boulevard, wondering despite the vague annoyance of a bullet in his brain if he was happier than he had ever been, and surprised himself by thinking of the farm for the first time in many months. He could borrow his brother's Impala and take the Sneering Brunette to the farm on their way to Nevada. He knew someone, the Japanese woman, who had recently been married in Elko. She was in San Francisco now, maybe they could stay with her for a while.

Spleen noticed that he had his hand on the butt of the gun that was tucked into his pants – suddenly a car turned its headlights on him.

He had the gun out by the time Billy Verité uttered, "Psst! Spleen – get in. I'll drive you."

"Christ, Billy. I guess she's got me spooked. I could've shot you."

All in all Spleen was pleased both with the dexterity with which he'd handled the gun – he had "whipped it out" – and with his apparent willingness to pull the trigger if necessary.

"Let me see the gun."

"Just drive. I'm going downtown, to the paper."

"All right, but I have to talk to you. You're in grave danger."

Spleen, who had felt in grave danger just a moment before, found that running the threat through the Billy Verité alembic made it seem a farce.

Spleen smiled.

Billy Verité shook his head grimly and shot onto the boulevard.

"It's true, Spleen. And you better listen to me and listen good. I hope that gun's loaded."

"It's loaded."

"Good. And you better be ready to use it."

"I'm ready to use it. Who's it you want dead?"

"Spleen, this is serious. Richie Buck's still in town and the last victim on the list is you. I've got it all figured out. How long has it been since you've seen me?"

It wasn't the kind of thing Spleen made it a point to keep track of.

"I don't know."

"I've been in hiding, see, in hiding. And I'll tell you why. Richie Buck and the cops are in cahoots. They have to be, otherwise it would be in the papers and no one would be dead except maybe Stratton who's not."

"Who's dead?"

"I can't prove it. That's the problem. I can't find the bodies."

"What bodies?"

"How long since you've seen Barlow?"

Spleen felt his forearms go numb. He waited for a chill to snake up or down his spine.

"Long time. I kind of forgot about him."

"Well, you can forget about him now."

Spleen stared at Billy's hideous mug, which he had forgotten about till he thought that this was how the news of a death was delivered, through a face that could be the laughing gates to hell.

"He's dead. I don't know where his body is, but he's dead."

"How do you know then if there's no body?"

Spleen winced at his own unenthusiastic, laborious skepticism. A mystery had been revealed to him, the hem of a cloak of a mystery you awake in the middle of the night to see slipping over the windowsill: the dead were more than the dead; he could feel the dead Barlow in the truth of Billy's idiotic words; Barlow the dead was communicating with him, telling him it was true.

"Because Gerard's missing, too."

"Gerard?"

"And a certain waitress who was the lover of, get this, none other than Detective Stratton."

"Why Gerard? How's he mixed up in this?"

"Stratton's partner, the black undercover cop. Gerard was messing with his girl."

"How long have all these – wait, the waitress – Sabatino's?"

"Right."

"Week nights?"

"That's the one."

"Christ."

"She was the last. Barlow's missing. As far as I can determine Gerard's missing. The waitress – "

"Three weeks."

"How'd you know?"

"I was there . . ."

"Now do you believe me?"

"Yes, but tell me what happened. How do you know all this? How are the cops involved?"

"Not the cops. Just Stratton and his partner. Stratton nabbed me while I was driving cab. On the North Side, in the alley by Zielke's. He questioned me about you."

"Me?"

"He thinks you killed Sherri Holloway. I figured it out. He said the biggest murder case in history and I remembered you were questioned and – "

"I killed Sherri Holloway? That was . . . six years ago.

What are they so hot about that now for?"

"Not they, Spleen. Stratton. He's a rogue cop and he's been after you since winter. He's convinced you killed her."

"He's been looking for me?"

"For months."

"He must be incompetent."

"He beat me and grilled me and I told him you weren't a killer, that it was that other guy, that Richie Buck they had to worry about, and just then Buck came up and knocked Stratton down and he was just going to strangle me to death when Stratton started pulling his gun so he had to let me go, and as soon as he did I fishtailed it out of there – "

"Hightailed."

"What?"

"Never mind. What happened next?"

"I don't know. I didn't stick around to find out. I went into hiding. You know there's an abandoned freight car by the Freighthouse Restaurant. It's all overgrown with weeds and the floor's gone; I've been staying there."

"How've you been making out? How've you been eating?"

"I had a little savings from driving cab. Plus there's the Network – but that's a secret. I'll tell you this, though, if you promise to keep it under your head."

"I promise."

"I found you and the dame because the desk clerk at her motel is in the Network. He didn't recognize her, but when he saw you last night – he saw you leaving – he contacted me."

"What about this conspiracy?"

"This is how I figure it, see. I watched the papers every

day after that to see if Buck killed Stratton, if there was a story about a missing cop or a dead cop. Or if Stratton got Buck, then it would be headline news: Cops Nab Fugitive. But I read the paper every day and there was no news at all, so I called the cops and asked for Stratton and when I found out he was there I hung up. I called him again later, but I'll get to that. See, I had to figure: I left a cop fighting a dangerous fugitive and if nothing came of it, see: what are the possibilities? One's dead or the other's dead or one's arrested. Right?"

"Or one got away and the other didn't want that known and so he hushed it up."

Billy Verité cocked his head like a dog and swerved over the center line and back into his lane.

"I never thought of that . . . But that's not how it went, so forget that. I had to wonder why nothing happened, and the only thing is they made some kind of deal, right? But why? Why would Stratton do it? Because of your connection with Barlow, I figure. I don't know why, but it's got to have something to do with that, 'cause I know Buck was here to kill Barlow and I know Stratton's after you. See? A connection."

"So you've known Stratton is after me for all this time and you're only warning me now?"

"I had to stay out of sight. I figured he'd be all over you, and I know he's after me because I'm the only witness that can connect him to Buck. I figured he'd have you in the slammer in a few days easy and you'd be found innocent and let go. I'm sorry, Spleen."

"Fine. Go on with your story. What did you do once you figured all this out?"

"I tried to find Barlow, to warn him. But he was already

gone. Then my sources told me Gerard was missing, too. See, another connection. He was shacking up with Stratton's partner's ex-girlfriend. Coincidence? Too many coincidences spoil the stew, pal. I don't buy it, not for a second. So next thing I do is call Stratton again and they say he's busy, so I say tell him it's a Mr. Buck, a Mr. R. Buck, and two seconds later Stratton's on the line and real quiet-like he says, just like this: What the fuck are you calling me here for? and I hang up. There's your proof, Spleen."

"What about the waitress?"

"When I heard about that I started looking real hard for you."

"Did you try my apartment?"

"Once. I snuck through the backyards late at night, but you weren't there so I figured you'd cleared out or maybe they got you already. But I kept looking just in case."

"They?"

"Stratton and his partner."

"I got word Buck was after me to break my legs."

"Who told you that?"

"The Fag With No Eyebrows snuck over one night to tell me."

"See? The cops have Buck doing their dirty work for them."

"Why would the cops want my legs broken?"

"To make you talk."

"I don't think it works that way. It's Deke Dobson – he wants his woman back."

"That's the other thing. Deke Dobson wants his woman back. He calls all the motels threatening the desk clerks if they hide her. Once a week at least to see if she's turned up. My guy at Weber's tells me every so often he'll drive up to check the register, look for her handwriting in case she's using an alias."

"Turn around. Go back to the motel."

Spleen suddenly felt as if a yam had somersaulted up from his stomach, lodging in his throat. They had just crossed Cass Street – it was five miles back to the motel. To panic would be ludicrous, he knew, but he was just getting used to his conviction and didn't want to waste it. If the Sneering Brunette were by his side every step of the way he could exercise his new resolve without fail – and he could shoot anybody who tried to take her away.

"She'll be there, Spleen. It's only been ten minutes."

"I know . . . You ever see the movie *Chinatown*?"

"No."

"Faye Dunaway shouts at the end about her dad, John Huston: He *owns* the police! I thought about it while you were talking before. Can't even go to the cops on this one, right? Stratton and the black undercover cop would shut you right up. No one would listen. They'd shut you up and turn you right over to Buck. You'd have been number four, instead of me."

Spleen noticed that he was the type to suddenly become loquacious when his anxiety was underscored by nobility. He shuddered as if beset by a cloud of fleas.

"See, I figured that out. I'm not as stupid as they think. I figured *them* out. They didn't figure *me* out."

Spleen felt the yam drop back down to his stomach at Billy's display of pride, the way it slapped gelatinously against the very real danger he knew the Sneering Brunette was in. He decided to resist his new loquacious self. He saw that Billy's mouth was still moving, and then his horse teeth when he stopped to smile, but his own tunnelment of thought caused the Doppler effecting of Billy's words, caused them to be projected then into the mouths of people on the street, into passing cars, onto signs advertising pizza and gas and liquor and car washes and the wrong motels; Billy's words shot out of the open window of the car like cigarettes that sparked when they bounced on the street behind them, while Spleen tried to figure out what bearing his anxiety would have on events. Would it be too late for the Sneering Brunette because he had panicked? Would his haste further confuse matters by preempting a display of cunning by the enemy? Was it leading him into a trap? Did a man of action have such feelings, or only a man of inaction who was trying to act? In which case, would he even recognize what he had botched? As they passed the last Joie de Gas on the way out of town he experienced a moment of calm and luxury, aware that he was being a fool in a way he seldom had a chance to be. He felt like someone who knew he'd finally gotten away with something that hadn't been proscribed in the first place. But then they reached the apex of the viaduct over the South Side railroad tracks and he could see below the motel that asserted itself in the spittle of light from its sign as a place where something most certainly was wrong. There was no movement, no activity, no sign of danger at all, just the weak pulsing of indifference, a throb that had access to Spleen's valve of discouragement, the way that an arrangement of objects has of notifying one of its indifference, and the significance that can only be had when there is something to be indifferent to.

"Shit," Spleen said without opening his teeth.

"What's wrong?"

"We're too late."

Billy Verité turned into the drive and drove around to the Sneering Brunette's room. The door was wide open and the light was still on. From the car Spleen could see the high-heeled shoe on the bed, and the bra on the lampshade beyond.

part three:

run in circles

7

. . . but I didn't take anything – I didn't, Jeff.
Won't you believe me?
  Baby, I don't care.

— Jane Greer and Robert Mitchum in
Out of the Past

I envy people who don't have to ignore the things that to me are horrendous impositions, like invasions of what little privacy I have, sardonic postcards from civilization sent to keep me up to date: this is what our music is like now; here's what the latest p.a. system sounds like; remember tuberculosis? It's back! I know people who have the ability to simply not hear the music from next door, even if it's the kind of music they hate. How can that not bother you? I'll ask when I visit someone who has a noise problem that would send me to Lafly's basement for a gun. I don't know, they'll say, it just doesn't. I wonder if these people were born with some kind of psychomental flux immunity, if they're immune to the insidiously mundane thoughts and sounds induced by civilization the same way so many others are immune to cancer. They're the ones who tell me simply to ignore the noise. And I try – the coughing will start and I'll meditate on something, or force myself to read; but there might as well be a small man who rides up through my brain on a dog to say hey, aren't you forgetting something? She's coughing – can't you hear that? And if I try to get through it by listening purposefully to the coughing, *accepting* it, there are more little men and more dogs. The cough will start and I'll envision the mucus escaping downwards, and a little conference at her larynx, the men deciding to send a team of sled dogs down to retrieve it. They never fail, and that's good for them, and good for her – the cougher – but I can't get any work done. I can't sleep. I can't fucking stand it.

Eight o'clock at night the coughing starts and by ten after I've tried everything. I'm out the door, headed for McDonald's. The place is crowded, not one empty booth. George Brown, a wiry old guy and still one of the fastest cabs in town, a gregarious maniac of a hack, is in a booth with Maynard, the security guard at the tech school who fancies himself something of a local historian. Rita's at a table surrounded by boys who still hide their tattoos from their parents and a couple of dropouts who sell drugs and have already learned how to look disinterested and keep their mouths shut. Rita looks bored. She's sixteen now – she soured on this burg years ago. She was on the pill when she was eleven, took part in orgies when she was twelve, busted out of the Lincoln Hills School for Girls that same year, turned tricks in Milwaukee until she was thirteen, returned here, persuaded one of her former foster fathers to hire a lawyer to prevent her being returned to the Home, and entered junior high school. Now there's a skinny kid who looks thirteen and twenty years younger than the basilisk gaze she turns on the hand he's slipped onto her breast. It looks like the hand crawled up there to die and she looks at it without scorn now, without pity, as if she and it are in collusion with a world of dry and timely fate. Rita has big brown eyes and chocolate skin and she would be beautiful if she didn't already look like you should have seen her when she was younger. I try a corner booth and a slab of hash browns leaps in my stomach when I see the red curly hair that used to bob sardonically around Sabatino's – it can't be, I think, and as it happens it's not, and I won't go into it. And of course the Parasite Lady is here – hello – and I could sit across from her, blow smoke up that little ass that doesn't – or does it? – function. The place is already on my nerves and I haven't even sat down. It doesn't make sense – the cougher should be here and I should be home. These aren't my people. Or are they? Are you my people? I want to scream it. George's and Maynard's lips going full speed at the same time; Rita now wedged between the two drug dealers, trying to extort a laugh out of herself; at least four furtive female schizophrenics I can count, all eager for the company of their own hostility; and – Oh Christ, there's one I can't let see me: got to be, Parasite Lady taken into account, the most repulsive woman on the planet: huge, rank, raunchy, her ever blue polyester stretch-pants sliding down salaciously to expose the crack of her ass, her ruddy pitted face, her mouth like fourteen São Paulo whores, and mean . . . I'm probably the only cab driver who ever got a tip out of her, I have that to be proud of, the time I drove her home from the Wonder

Bar, three or four blocks, and she must have propositioned me nine different ways, none subtle, and when we pulled up at her house I told her I was sorry but I didn't have a penis, and her laugh came like a sandpaper projectile launched from dry bowels, and she gave me an extra quarter. So I choose a seat without much more ado, in a booth across from Bette Davis, who looks up from an enormous biography of Marlon Brando, and I think now I'm in for it, two hours I'll have to listen to him talk about Marlon Brando; that's how it often is, him cornering me, my head lolling, arms flailing, as wave after wave of information lifted from some book and run through his latest persona comes at me. And if it's not that, it'll be some variation of our other conversation, the same one we've been having for years, always with the same antipodal inclinations, his optimism, my pessimism. I get my attitude, I suppose, from being around too many people, and getting too close to a select few who disappoint me by telling themselves the same lies I keep hidden; he gets his from watching movies, staying away from people. As far as I know he has no friends, no one ever sits with him at McDonald's. I want him to know what people are like; I want him to know that his naivete is like that of a general overseeing a battle from on top of a hill. But when I enumerate for him the components of the lies that people live he wraps a movie around it and revels in the same tragedy that makes me want to vomit in the laughing faces of youth and beauty; I can convince him that perversity is the last refuge of truth, but it only incites him – he'll think of a movie, a character, a noble carrier of this or that perversion. I don't know who's wrong and who's right, but I know that before long, despite myself, I'll get caught up in it with him (one of my own perversions, perhaps); yes, I'll say, I saw it, too, she was perfect for that role; and

[169]

soon enough I'm at his house and we're watching the movie, and I don't fully understand why I'm grateful for the tragedy . . .

But I won't have any of his Brando lectures, I tell him right off, I've heard it all before, and besides, all you need to know you can see in *Last Tango,* and to top it off I say if you want to talk about actors talk about Sterling Hayden, the greatest actor of all time. Usually if you want to shut people up all you have to do is take things to extremes, but Bette just expresses his disagreement mildly; he's bemused, his legs crossed, managing to keep his back straight, yet leaning forward as if he's trying not to pee – the best a man can do sometimes without an operation. He's lost a lot of weight since he adopted this new, feminine persona – his smile with all the wrinkles is like a white stone dropped into a pool – and he truly has the mannerisms down, especially with the cigarette. Sometimes I have to remind him that there are places he won't want to be doing that, like certain taverns. I would've thought union meetings, too – he works for the brewery; he's a *Teamster* – but I asked and he told me of course he holds his cigarette this way at the meetings, he believes in being a lady twenty-four hours a day. Maybe you only get beat up if you're too provocative, if you make them want you too bad. As Bette goes on about Sterling Hayden (yes, he knows all about Sterling Hayden – I didn't know that Hayden had been in the OSS and that that's how he became a Red, working with the Yugoslav resistance; nor did I know that Joan Crawford wanted to bed him during the filming of *Johnny Guitar,* and that she was such a bitch about how many lines Mercedes McCambridge got, that the whole thing disgusted and disillusioned Hayden), I wonder how all his characters would have responded to Bette. Johnny Guitar would've slapped him on the ass and made pleasant, if lewd, comments. I think the gangster he played in *Asphalt Jungle*, the one who tells his gal to make the coffee or shut up about it, would've been detached, shown a momentary, baffled interest and moved on. Roger Wade in *The Long Goodbye* would get Bette drunk, try in his extravagant way to get to the bottom of things, ask difficult questions, grab his wrist and make him sit down again. The peasant Dalco in *1900* would take to the fields amused, yet another reason to be glad he's not rich enough to lose his bearings. The only one Bette would have to fear would be Sergeant McClusky from *The Godfather*, who'd like to get at him with a broom handle for reasons made clear by Freud. But suddenly he's on Robert Mitchum, not Sterling Hayden, Robert Mitchum in *Out of the Past*. I see what he's doing – he knows I don't want to talk about Spleen. You transparent bitch, I want to say, I know what you're up to and it's not going to work, you're not going to get me to talk about it. I think about leaving, but I look around and there's the crowd again, there's Rita sitting across from the Parasite Lady, an overly serious expression on her face, obviously mocking her; Rita's friends are watching, some holding their hands over their mouths, trying to contain their laughter, while others try to expand theirs to contain their boredom. And Bette drones on about Jane Greer's charming deceit: Mitchum wants to believe her, even the audience does. We know she's lying, but we want her to trick us, we want to be taken in by her lies.

"Everybody except Kirk Douglas," I say. "He wants her to be bad. He wants to watch her lie and know she's lying. It arouses him."

"It arouses us."

"In a different way. In the end we wish she wasn't bad, if only for Mitchum's sake."

"But Mitchum knew what he was getting into. As soon as he said, 'Baby, I don't care.' No, we didn't care about him after that. We knew what was coming and really would not have been satisfied if it happened any other way. In your terms, she's the perversion we want to see acted out. If they let us down, if they let her be good, we'd be outraged."

"Strange, isn't it? We want Mitchum to be strong, to show us a way out . . ."

"That's why we watch movies, to escape – "

"No. No, that's not what I mean. And I think you're wrong, anyway. We only do it for escape if that's all they give us. What *I* really want is a hero, a Jesus, someone to tell me how to live. But if Mitchum made it, if he won – if he got the good girl and lived, I'd be suspicious. So I guess you're right about that, I think I want him to make it but I really don't. I'd be suspicious and I'd be watching the movie to escape because I know it's not that way. Mitchum would mean nothing to me. But he does mean something. He's Noir Man, he walks the line between the only two ways out I know of – complete acceptance (the hedonist), and complete rejection (the monk). Noir Man takes the sublime out of cynicism, brings cynicism down to Earth where it belongs; and he accepts one thing, a case, a woman – he doesn't accept everything. He rejects almost everything – he's not a fool – but he can't go monking after the vapors because he doesn't even believe in his own soul. The only reason he believes in anything is because he tells himself he has to or he can't act, and something he quits bothering to try to identify in his guts tells him he has to act

. . . or he might as well. Do you get what I'm telling you? It's tragedy – Noir Man is the only way the man of our civilization can accept tragedy and live with it. And we have to do that or we're deluded, absolute egoists, idiots. If we lose our tragic sense, we lose our resistance. Noir Man is the new fatalist. So you're right, we don't want Mitchum to come out on top, not in a way we can't believe – but we wouldn't mind if he did in a way that would make sense . . . "

Bette laughed, but not snidely enough to offend me into leaving.

"That was a pretty speech," he said, tossing his head as if a nest of auburn curls would uncoil, "but I'm somewhat easier to please. I ask to be transported, not saved."

"I ask not to want to be transported."

"You ask for Robert Mitchum to live for you, to come down off the screen and cut a swath through your future. But he can't, there's that 'Baby, I don't care.'"

"Yes. That 'Baby, I don't care.' What a commitment. He doesn't say yes, does he? Or no, but. Just 'Baby, I don't care.'"

"A very Christian act. He suspends all moral judgment of her in asserting his own morality. His morality *is* the acceptance of her."

I see that one of the drug dealers has joined Rita in the Parasite Lady's booth. Across the aisle one of the schizoid gals is listening to every word, an expression on her face like there's a turd on a plate in front of her. While I'm looking around the Fag With No Eyebrows comes in carrying a paper shopping bag. It looks like something's moving inside it. Suddenly the lights that came on outside have gone off, causing more of an atmospheric shift than a deprivation of light – we've always got plenty in here – a claustrophobic suggestion that soon no air will be available. We all look out there, but it's only the mayflies. This is their night.

I wish I didn't have to see any of these people, but I have to get out sometimes – to tell the truth, I think it's more involved than fleeing the cougher. And miserable as it is here, my only *real* fear is that for some reason Spleen Two will walk in, the last person on the planet I want to see. Nothing personal. I like what I know of him. He's generous, apparently, all that money he gave Spleen, and the car he loaned him without pressing for too thorough an explanation. He would like to be of more help, he said. But Spleen said no, it wouldn't do to get him involved.

"So what did the cops say?" Spleen asked.

"They wouldn't say much. You know how they are, they want you to do the talking. They'll ask the questions. They mostly wanted to know where you live. I told them they could go fuck themselves. Stratton wanted to beat the hell out of me, but the black guy held him back. Something's way out of bounds there . . . Do you know what's going on?"

Spleen looked at his brother, trying to feel that peculiar displacement he imagined one felt when confronted by one's doppelganger, or would feel if the image in the mirror moved its lips independently. But he felt nothing extraordinary. It was just his brother, just another human, one who looked like *he* was supposed to look.

"They think I killed Sherri Holloway. *You* didn't do it by any chance, did you?"

"Again?"

"I think it's just them, those two. They're nuts. It'll go away."

"This have anything to do with why you want the car?"

"Probably not. I hope not."

"Why don't we go to the cops right now, different cops, and get the whole thing out in the open?"

"I can't right now, but soon, all right?"

"Sure."

Spleen Two grimaced pleasantly. Spleen wondered if he made the same face. He tried, and found it awkward.

"You sure you know what you're doing?"

"No."

"That's a relief. I don't know what I'd think if you were certain of anything."

Spleen smiled at him, thinking that each of them was the older brother in his own way.

"Seen Pop?"

"Every other week or so."

"He still ask about me?"

"No. I tell him I'm you sometimes. That appeases him."

"Thanks."

"It's better than having him see the two of us at once."

"How do you think he managed while we were growing up?"

"I don't think he did. I think he still doesn't know what hit him."

Spleen chuckled.

"So you think it was us?"

"Nah. He was already that way. But when you think about it: all those cows that look alike and then the same with his kids . . . Can't be easy for a simpleton."

"Well, is he happy?"

"No. He's not happy at all."

Spleen stood up, picking the car keys off the table.

"Thanks," he said. "I'll get back to you as soon as I can."

Near the McDonald's door the sleeves of a suit jacket slid up two skinny arms all the way to the elbows. Between them a hat rested on top of two ears. A newspaper covered the face that was somewhere below the hat. Spleen stopped and dipped his head down over the paper.

"All right, Billy. Call Detective Stratton in exactly five minutes and tell him you just saw me parked down at Riverside in a blue Impala."

"Check."

The drive at Riverside Park was a one-way horseshoe made into an oval by State Street, which led down to it. Spleen turned off State onto the drive and followed it around to the river. A strip of grass lay next to the drive; rocks sloped beyond it to the water. He pulled up next to a tree that was surrounded by pigeons and ducks. The birds were fattening themselves on loaves of bread someone had recently tossed there for them. The birds observed no clear pattern of segregation, but a wariness prevailed. When a duck and pigeon both eyed the same chunk of bread, they would circle slowly, watching each other, the pigeon bobbing its head, the duck falling to the side and catching itself, falling to the side and catching itself, circling until one or the other looked away long enough to spot a different chunk. Seconds after Spleen pulled up, a blue jay landed gracelessly on a low, dying branch of the tree and began limping spasmodically back and forth. Spleen gave the jay what was intended to be a dull once-over, but when it saw it had Spleen's attention it began whistling fervently, hopping clumsily on the branch.

"Crazy fucking bird," Spleen mumbled, and then saw it suddenly pitch forward winglessly. The ducks and pigeons beneath scattered, and the blue jay landed with a damp thud. The others quickly closed on it, found it dead and not to their taste, and went back to the desultory pursuit of bread.

Spleen figured that if Billy Verité got hold of him, Stratton would be along any minute. He didn't expect Buck to be with him, but kept the Ivers-Johnson by his side anyway. There weren't enough trees in the park to block his view of the cars turning in, though he wasn't sure if he could make out the features of those driving. Luckily there weren't too many cars to choose from. The first was a station wagon driven by a woman. After a minute or two, after the station wagon had made it around and passed Spleen, a van with lettering on the side appeared, a good bet for an undercover vehicle. Spleen held the key in the starter – but the van halted directly across the park from him. He saw the figure of a man lurch toward the passenger side, then bob back up, open his door, and leap out. He wore white overalls and was very fat. Then Spleen saw a woman, equally fat, rise above the van, waddling up a knoll. Her head disappeared over the knoll before the man reached it. Spleen, wondering if he'd be able to follow the chase beyond the knoll, if they'd eventually come back into view, noticed a third vehicle out of the corner of his eye. It was a maroon sedan, lacking the rear antenna that would have been a dead giveaway. The driver, though, was clearly looking in Spleen's direction when his left front tire climbed the curb. It was Stratton, all right, trying to remain calm, to make the car appear unassuming as its left front tire rejoined the drive.

At the exact moment Spleen ignited his engine, the pigeons took to the air, leaving the ducks to their bread. Spleen looked up at the Cass Street Bridge. No one leaped. He looked in his rearview mirror, then tilted it so he could see the tip of the Island. No figure sat on a rock. He readjusted the mirror, catching a glimpse of the maroon sedan making the first turn. It was time to move. He gauged Stratton's speed at 15 mph and held the Impala there. Stratton didn't seem to be accelerating. Spleen remembered the pigeons and looked out for them, seeing one or two arcing in and out of his sight. At the turn back onto State Street, Spleen accelerated to 20 mph, and by the time he reached the turn back onto the drive he knew that Stratton aimed to keep up, but not overtake him. Halfway down the straightaway he saw a green Nova across the park from him, as far behind Stratton as Stratton was behind him. When he lurched to 25 at the next turn, the flock of pigeons swung into view – they were circling over his car. Turning into the second straightaway, back alongside the river, he had a good view of the field – both cars were maintaining speed. He gradually dropped to 20 and both cars did the same. The Nova had to be Buck. Reaching State Street he considered heading straight out of the park – how long would they simply follow him in circles? – but when the turn back onto the drive presented itself he couldn't resist, and as he turned he leaned his head out the window to see the thirty pigeons circling in the sky directly above. As Spleen approached the van he saw two heads rise over the knoll. The van said "Cavendish Paints." When he was even with it he saw the couple from the waist up, their arms on each others' shoulders. Both cars made the turn behind him. Alongside the river again he remembered the gun and reached for it without looking. It wasn't there. Looking along the seat, he saw the wood butt sticking up between the seat and the door and leaned across for it. Steering with his left hand, he let his right get used to the gun. At the turn onto State he looked back and saw the sedan and the Nova following dutifully. At the turn back onto the drive he had to brake for a carload of teenagers which snuck in ahead of him, a few of the kids calling out the windows, telling Spleen to fuck himself. He was only one man and they were many, but he was a man with a gun and he pointed it at their car, which accelerated suddenly and nearly sideswiped the van that was hoping to pull back into the middle of the drive. The van waited for Spleen to pass as well. Once he saw that Stratton and Buck had turned onto the drive again, Spleen accelerated to 30. Stratton jumped the curb to get around the van. Ahead, the car the teenagers were in fishtailed after taking the last turn, gained control of itself, and sped straight back toward downtown. Leaving the river behind again, Spleen looked back to see the Nova slide effortlessly past the van, which had stopped. Should Spleen make another round? Yes. He glanced at the sky again: the pigeons were still there. He slowed to 15; the enemy slowed to 15. Spleen had flushed them out, but so far they were unwilling to show their hand. What did it mean that they were content to follow him around the park? Were they waiting for Spleen to blunder into a less public place? Spleen put the gun back on the seat and gripped the wheel with both hands. What were the pigeons going to do? Would they follow him out of the park? He came alongside the river yet again and thought to look for the blue jay. It lay belly-up next to the tree. The ducks were giving it a wide berth. At the next opportunity to leave the park, Spleen again resisted when he saw a Cadillac about to turn. An old man was driving and Spleen recognized him. It was Mr. Zafar, owner of the oldest clothing store in the city. Spleen raced in ahead of him, then slowed to Zafar's speed, about 10 mph. If Stratton and Buck turned in he had them duped, at least enough to gain a few seconds. When Stratton turned Spleen accelerated to 15, fast enough so that Stratton would be able to catch up to Zafar, but not so fast that he'd panic into passing him. When Buck pulled in Spleen smiled. By the time he turned onto State, Stratton was as far back as Buck had been. Old Zafar was holding up his end. Spleen flicked on his left turn signal just to make it look good as he approached the entrance to the park, and floored the gas pedal, shooting straight up to Front Street, making a screeching left turn, taking the next right at Vine, and the next left at Second Street, which took him between a row of factories before curving up to the intersection where the Causeway arrived downtown. The Causeway was the first of two main arteries parallel to the river lead-ing to the North Side; it ran five lanes wide and straight for the first mile – Spleen would be able to see the maroon sedan and the green Nova turn on behind him when he was halfway across, Stratton and Buck, side by side, no doubt bearing down on him – sloping from downtown into the valley where industry kept the marsh at bay, refusing the timid La Crosse River its delta. Ahead of Spleen the Causeway hooked to the right, then rose over the North Side viaduct. He calculated that he'd be out of the enemy's sight for about twenty seconds. He made the curve and took the first left, onto Car Street, and turned into the alley that cut through to Holstein. He counted to thirty before turning onto Holstein, back onto the Causeway, and climb-ing the viaduct, from where he saw that he was now following his pursuers. He followed at a distance of two blocks, hoping traffic between would cover him, or that

Stratton and Buck simply wouldn't look back. They were taking it slow, looking for the Impala up and down side streets. After a mile they gave up, Stratton accelerating and Buck pulling in behind him. They turned on Loomis, and eventually Spleen followed suit, just in time to see the back end of the Nova disappear into the alley on the second block. Spleen turned into the first alley, raced through to Sturgeon, and waited long enough to make sure that they had stopped somewhere in that alley. He backed up until he reached the rear of Cavendish Paints, where he parked the Impala between two vans.

The daylight was broad. Spleen stuffed the gun in the front of his pants and untucked his shirt to cover the butt. The pigeons were making a swift, tight circle in the sky above. Spleen hoped the pigeons would stay with the car rather than follow him.

North Siders, generally, could not afford fences. Spleen walked swiftly through to Avon Street. Somewhere in the alley behind the row of houses across the street, Buck and Stratton were parked, unless they'd gone into a house, in which case they could have been looking out a picture window at him as he crossed the street, perhaps training rifles on him (with scopes). Spleen crept alongside a one-story green house that had its front door open and an array of bicycles upturned on a lawn beleaguered by desertification. He kept his eye on the alley he could see only in brief stretches where garages didn't obstruct his view. When he reached the rear of the house he saw the back end of the maroon sedan behind the garage of the next house. He sidled with his back to the house until he came upon an old woman rounding the corner. Before she could exclaim, Spleen put his finger to his lips. The woman was barefoot and carried a spatula that looked as if it had been chewed by a dog. She looked blankly at Spleen, pointing the spatula at his midsection. His shirt had gotten hung up on the butt of the gun. "I might not have to use it if you keep quiet," he said. Her expression did not betray her immediate intentions; her eyes narrowed as if hankering after a noncommittal sun setting past a hopeful horizon. The garage was right off the alley, separate from the house. Spleen went into a crouch and made a dash for it. It was stucco, and Spleen wondered why. He wondered, too, what made him think Stratton and Buck were in there. Then he heard a banging like two hundred pounds tossed into three trash cans, and felt the entire garage vibrate when a quiet thump followed. The old woman had followed Spleen across the yard silently; she stood a few feet to his left, staring. There was an open window on her side of the garage, and Spleen moved past her to crouch under it; inside he could hear the struggle subdue itself. He looked back at the woman as he listened. She just stood there. It made him uncomfortable and he looked up for the pigeons. They weren't there.

"All right," a voice inside the garage panted, "all right."

"You won't want to talk that way to me anymore."

The second voice had a great deal more authority than the first.

"No."

"You're sorry."

There was a pause and then a sound like a rodent underfoot.

"You're sorry."

"Yes, yes – sorry," the first voice said, urgent and laryngitic.

"Good. I'll ask again: Was that Spleen?"

"Yes."

"I want you to lay off. He's my problem."

"You – you didn't mention him. I didn't know. He's a suspect in a murder case. I need to question him."

"You won't be able to do that."

"Why – why not?"

"Spleen's a dead man."

Spleen assumed the old woman was listening, too. He pointed his thumb at his chest and mouthed: That's me.

No response registered.

"No."

"What?"

Spleen heard the rodent noise again.

"What?"

"Yes, but wait. Did Dobson hire you to kill him? I'll talk to Dobson. I need Spleen alive. I'll get Dobson to pay you and you can go. You'll be done. You can collect your money and – "

Something made Stratton decide to shut up. He grunted instead.

Spleen had heard enough. Motioning for the old woman to follow, he retreated to Avon Street. The pigeons still circled in the sky, lest he forget where he'd parked his car. Feeling safe again, he looked behind him for the old woman. She wasn't there. He pictured her still standing by the garage holding her dog-chewed spatula. Going back for her seemed a bad idea. Besides, Buck wouldn't kill an old lady in broad daylight, would he?

Phase One of Spleen's action plan was a success. He'd flushed the enemy out and tricked them into betraying their intentions. Perhaps he should have plugged them both right there in the garage; but then where would that have left the Sneering Brunette? Still in the clutches of Deke Dobson, that's where.

"This is Deke Dobson."
  "Deke."
  "Who is this?"
  "This is Deke Dobson?"
  "Yes goddamnit, who is this?"
  "This is *Deke Dobson*."
  "Who the fuck – "
  "Deke? This is Spleen."

There was a long pause, then Dobson's voice again, cunning with subdued triumph, like a cat stumbled upon a crippled mouse.

  "Spleen . . . nice to hear from you. I've been wanting to meet you for a long time . . ."
  "That's why I'm calling."
  "Wonderful. When can you come over?"
  "Not there. Someplace where I can see you haven't brought that goon along. I want him off my back . . . I'm willing to pay."
  "Sure, sure, I think we can work something out. Where would you like to meet?"

"Petitbone Park, by the swing sets. Either walk or take a cab. I don't want to see any cars. Be there at 8:45. I'll be there either before or after that, but you be there exactly at 8:45. Alone."

Petitbone Park was across the river from Riverside Park. Like Riverside it had few trees in it. The only place to hide a green Nova would be behind the octagonal gazebo that squatted some five hundred yards past the swing sets. If Spleen followed the drive all the way around so his car would be pointed toward the park's exit, poised for escape, he'd see it. Instead, he drove right up onto the grass, pulled up next to Dobson and left the car running while he executed his plan, which was to run directly to Dobson with a smile on his face that could be seen for five hundred yards, even in the crepuscular gloom. Dobson was too stunned by Spleen's hearty approach to respond; he let Spleen run right up to him and slap him on the shoulders repeatedly, managing only to murmur variations of phrases like "What the fuck?" and "Are you crazy?" Even when Spleen shouted "It worked!" loud enough to be heard six hundred, seven hundred yards away, the best Dobson could do was take a step back and conjure with his mouth an effeminate rendition of disgust. He just didn't get it. Now Spleen was jumping up and down in front of him, waving his arms, shouting, "You tricked him! You're a genius!" and when he stopped that he pulled out an Ivers-Johnson .22 pistol, showed it to Dobson, threw his arms around Deke, and retreated to his car as the Nova pulled out from behind the gazebo and headed straight for where Deke Dobson stood with his brows furrowed, watching Spleen drive across the grass, turning back to witness the Nova's new intentions bearing down on him just in time to dive out of the way. As Spleen's Impala bounced onto the drive, he looked back to see Dobson running for the cover of a hackberry tree and Buck turning to make another run at him. Phase Two of his action plan, it seemed, had worked.

It was almost completely dark now. The streetlights were on, mayflies beginning to riot around them. There always had to be something in the air. The pigeons had followed his car until he crossed the Cass Street Bridge, now it was the mayflies. It was a late hatch, which usually meant there would be a lot of them. He crossed the bridge back into the city, expecting the pigeons to greet him, but there was only the gathering frenzy of the mayflies around every light.

Spleen entered Dobson's house through the unlocked back door with his gun drawn. Phase Three was going to have to be taken quite seriously. A faint light from the living room exposed the contours of the obstacles in the kitchen. He stopped to look around, expecting to find henchman all over the living room, but there was only the Fag With No Eyebrows curled in his chair reading a magazine. Spleen was on him in two quiet seconds, squeezing his ear with his thumb and forefinger and forcing the barrel of the gun past his teeth. The Fag With No Eyebrows gagged. "Don't make another sound," Spleen said, "except to tell me where she is." The Fag indicated upstairs with his eyes. "Make a sound and I'll come back down and kill you. Now don't move from this chair." He started to move away, then turned back, forgetting himself and asking conversationally, "Anybody else up there?"

The Fag With No Eyebrows now looked more bewildered than frightened. He shook his head. The Sneering Brunette was alone.

Spleen climbed the stairs quickly. He had no idea how long it would take Buck to finish off Dobson and come after him. At the top of the stairs he saw only one room dropping light into the hallway. From the doorway he saw her on a rocking chair, facing a small television with people moving inside it. Her back was to him. She was wearing a black slip and he could tell right off that she'd washed her hair earlier in the day. He looked at her arms to see if they were bound to the chair, but he detected no sign at all that she was a captive.

She crossed her legs and leaned back in her chair, tossing her head Spleen's direction, but not far enough that she could see him.

"Is that you, hon?" she asked. Her voice was languid and genuine. "How'd it go?"

"I guess you're not going to think it went very well."

She leaped sideways out of the chair, contorting in the air so that she landed on her knees facing Spleen.

"Spleen!"

Spleen's wry smile was barely perceptible.

"I came to save you."

"Spleen? I – don't know what to say . . ."

"Take your time. I'm kind of busy running things through my head trying to figure out where I got it wrong."

"You came to save me," she repeated mechanically, her voice trailing off. "You – you have a mayfly on your shirt."

She was looking at his shoulder. He plucked the mayfly off gently, despite what for it must have been a tenacious struggle to remain there. He tossed it into the air and it fluttered in loops toward the window screen, where it stuck.

The Sneering Brunette stood and crossed before Spleen to the bed. She sat on the edge and looked up at him.

Then she looked at the gun and asked, "Did you kill Deke?"

Spleen had forgotten the gun. He looked down at it as if it had grown there recently.

"No. I think Buck did. Or is. Or will . . . So you're not a captive?"

She shook her head.

"After I left I came right back and found out he'd taken you. I figured – "

"I called him, Spleen. Right after you left."

Spleen felt melodramatic.

"Her vice is honesty," he said softly.

"I'm sorry, Spleen."

"I guess."

"It's not the way I wanted it."

"You called him. You asked him to come get you?"

"I didn't see any other way."

"There might have been one."

"I couldn't stand it anymore."

"Sure. It's a case of bad timing. But now what?"

"Now?"

"Now. Buck could be here any minute, depending on what he chooses to do with the body. If he decides to take it and bury it in the woods it could take hours. My guess is he'll nudge it into the river with his foot. Then he'll come after me. The first place he'll look is here. I'd like to get you out of here before I meet up with him, unless of course you've really gone over to the enemy."

The Sneering Brunette's eyes filled with tears, and she slumped forward, her elbows on her thighs and her hair covering her face. She looked like a housewife who at three in the afternoon said fuck it, one more glass of sherry. She looked like Anne Bancroft wearily trying to persuade Dustin Hoffman to come back to bed so she could hate them both a little more.

The man of action is an idealist, but so is the woman who cries for a bad man.

"I'm being too callous about his death," Spleen guessed.

She lifted her head, drawing the hair back from in front of her eyes.

"No matter who he was, Spleen, I slept with him. I

touched his flesh. He washed my nipples in the shower. He was a man, Spleen. He was alive and he touched my body."

The weakest words in the language were trying to back their way out of Spleen's mouth: what . . . about . . . me? He swallowed and felt light-headed, taking a step backward to keep from pitching over like a dead blue jay. He saw himself from across the room, in front of the closet in which the things she wore must have been hung, the dresses Spleen liked, and her black slips. He looked ridiculous – the gun was the size of a cannon.

"You're not coming with me then, are you?"

"I have nothing to fear here."

Her eyes were red, but there were no more tears.

Spleen regretted that there were moments to endure that would be filled with the flux of remembered events, never comprehensible in the first place, that could only be arranged without hierarchy, and only be banished by a futile gesture.

But they heard the back screen door slam and they tensed and waited, Spleen determining that his urge to lay the bloody corpse of a man across her bare feet was without honor, heard the Fag With No Eyebrows screech, and then a heavy, dull slap –

When I was a boy, I stayed at my friend Billy's house, and I woke up in the middle of the night to the angry curses of Billy's stepfather and the frightened pleading of his mother. There was a window right next to my bed, and when I heard Billy say to his stepfather, "Put the shotgun down," I looked it over to see how it opened, in case the shooting started and I had to get out of there fast. There were long periods of silence when I didn't know what was going on and I was scared shitless and kept looking at the window wanting to get the hell out of there, but afraid that if I made any noise he'd come in and kill me. I wondered if I could get out quick enough, if I got out and ran if I would make it or get shot in the back, or get shot while fumbling at the window. Then the cursing and pleading and Billy's pathetic appeals would rise and make enough noise to cover any sound I might make, but I'd be too afraid to move. I heard Billy's stepfather say, "Where are *you* going?" and his mother answer, whimpering, "To the hospital," and then a loud smack, and after the smack a very long pause, and finally the crumply thud of her body hitting the floor. And that's what I want more than anything to get across, that pause, the meaning of it, that delay, after the smack and before the thud. If I could only get across the meaning of that time, that hiatus, that wait . . . none of the words, even, are appropriate; there is no word for it . . . But there is a meaning to it and I want to go on and on about it, for it is in me somewhere, I've comprehended it, I've swallowed it. But I give up. It means everything, or everything it means is . . . I can't. There's no expressing it.

– and then the thump of his body hitting the floor.

"The window," the Sneering Brunette said, rushing over to lift the screen.

Feet were ascending the stairs.

The mayfly rode up with the screen.

Spleen climbed out the window, clinging to the sill with his hands, extending slowly into a dangle. When he was at full length he looked up at the Sneering Brunette.

"Don't get killed," she said.

Spleen looked below: nothing between his feet and the ground.

It was a long way down.

part four:

scream and shout

8

The sound of implosion is screaming.

— Ava Gardner to her psychiatrist in
Committed

A mile from the river people walk into their houses covered with mayflies – having walked just from the car to the front door. When all the mayflies hatch at once there isn't a light between the bluffs and the river that isn't under some degree of swarm. The closer to the river, the more mayflies. Half a mile away the intersections are nearly impassable, and downtown it's impossible to drive. They tried changing the lights along the Cass Street Bridge from white to yellow, but when the mayflies are out in force enough of them don't care what color they die under that the bridge still has to be closed. A few years ago, the bridge was repaved with iron grating for better mayfly traction or something, but that didn't help either.

A lot of people are horrified by the mayflies, the sheer number of them, the way they stick to you, their inconceivable anatomy, what they hope to suggest by their short life cycle. Under the lights downtown the dying and the dead are a foot deep, a swarming, yet lethargic carpet. They're dying anyway, but for some people it's unpleasant to be unable to take a step without taking a life, without hearing, or feeling – you can't tell – that light crunch underfoot.

These last two years all the lights downtown went dark. Thick clouds of mayflies went berserk around them, completely covering them and then some. Between lights strings of mayflies formed, going from one to the other. Beneath the lights vertical strings formed as well, mayflies dropping from the clouds, and always those escaping from the death mass below popping up and trying to make it back to the cloud. Within hours of the first hatchings the streets were coated with them and the city had effectively shut down. Those who loved mayflies, the docility they displayed individually, their lovely transparent wings, the desperate hope of their ludicrous lives, walked through the streets as if it were the first snowfall of the new winter. It's amazing to walk on a carpet of mayflies, amazing to be covered from head to foot by hundreds of harmless, weightless insects. You can pluck them off yourself and throw them at someone and they'll stick. But starting last year it eventually became difficult to breathe outside, there were so many of them. They'd inevitably get in your mouth, and your nostrils, and all around your eyes. By midnight last year you couldn't cross the street downtown without being blinded and losing your way. It's too late, we're too far from biblical times, for there to be talk of plague, yet for one day a year at least the same kind of fear – encouraged by a guilty knowledge somewhere too deep inside to locate that something has been violated or this wouldn't be happening, a sick feeling akin to that which occurs when haste leads to something irremediable, irreversible – our ancestors must have experienced lingers in the hushed air closed off from the air outside alive with mayflies. Maybe it will get worse every year and these insects that live only for a day will eventually bring down our civilization. I look around at the fear – even Bette goes silent; and the schizophrenics aren't talking to themselves – and I smile at the thought. I get up and go to the window: it's dark out and there is no sky but when I look carefully I can see that it's not a plague, just a bunch of goddamn mayflies.

Spleen had about a dozen mayflies on his head alone by the time he reached his car outside Dobson's house, but the worst was yet to come. The bridges weren't yet closed and the streets nearest the river were just beginning to get slippery. When he hit the downtown some light still escaped through the death dance of the mayflies. He could not have realized how bad the storm was going to get.

Through downtown and halfway across the Causeway Spleen knew Richie Buck was behind him like he knew the back of a hand that had crawled up out of a sewer and into his life. He was headed for the Island, which from his blue heron days he knew like the back of a more benign hand. His plan was simple. There was a dead-end road on the south end of the Island, on the other side of the railroad tracks. The road snaked into the woods and narrowed into a trail. He would park at the end of the road and ambush Buck. The Nova would pull up behind the Impala, Buck would start to get out, and Spleen would blast him, with all eight bullets, from close range; from behind a tree, he would step out and blast him. Phase Four.

It would only work if he kept enough distance between the Impala and the Nova, so he kept his speed up to ten miles per hour over the limit, which nearly meant disaster when he turned too swiftly onto the Island bridge road, which was already coated by mayflies, and lost control of the car. The Impala did a long and graceful full turn, fishtailed for a hundred feet, and continued ahead, Spleen checking the rearview mirror for the Nova. He didn't want Buck to gain too much distance and he didn't want him to crash. Buck had gained some since the Causeway, but he took the turn even faster than Spleen and slammed the Nova nearly sideways into the guardrail; the back end hit after a long slide, jarring the car back into the proper forward position, yet slowing Buck down enough so that his tires spun on the mayflies and Spleen was able to regain the distance he'd lost.

Bainbridge Street was not lit well enough to appeal to the earliest mayflies and Spleen was able to drive with his head out the window – the windshield was opaque from the dead – without any of them hitting his eyes. The Impala got up to 75 mph before Spleen slammed on the brakes too late to slow down for the railroad tracks. His eyes had teared up from the wind and he was flying in a car through the air; in a moment he would land somewhere, and he understood the inextricable presence of doom in suspension; the car landed on the road and bounced, the rear end scraping the pavement, sending out sparks, the gun digging into his back to remind him of his mission. He was able to slow enough to make the turn onto the dirt road, his head still uncertain how close it was to the ground. There was no looking back for the Nova now. He drove as fast as he deemed safe, until there was no more room.

The noise outside the car was bizarre and maddening. Spleen couldn't identify it. It was partly like a roar of damp applause, partly like a shower of paper clips. It threatened him with abstraction. He walked into the woods, slapping mayflies out of the way of his face, feeling besieged by the sound. He wanted to close his hands over his ears and scream. It was worse than being tuned in to your own heartbeat. He got behind a wide hackberry tree about ten feet from the road, from where he had a clear view of the space behind the Impala, where Buck would soon be parked. Annoyed, he took the gun out of his pants and slapped it through the air, swatting several mayflies. One landed under his nostril and he plucked it off, suddenly realizing what the noise was. The slough was nearby and hundreds of thousands of mayflies were hatching, popping out of the water, and the fish were feeding on them, thousands of fish flopping around, leaping, slapping back into the water. And the paper clips were the mayflies in the air, thousands of little wings clapping amidst the trees. He looked up. He couldn't see far into the darkness, but what he could see was similar to the illusion of a forest: close up there seems to be plenty of space, but the further in you look, the less space – yet you know it's the same space. But Spleen didn't know, and it seemed the blackness was a blanket of mayflies overhead. The noise was tolerable now that he knew what it was, but he yearned to see a single star overhead and could not find one. He couldn't even see the tops of most trees. He checked his car – he could barely make out its outline from ten feet away. He wondered how close Buck could get without him hearing. It had already been too long, he figured; he couldn't expect Buck to pull up obliviously with his lights on. So Buck suspected an ambush. What would he do? He might block the road with his car, so escape by Impala was out. Spleen thought of running fast and far through the woods, but sheer accident could lead him right into Buck. Besides, he remembered, he knew this place and Buck didn't. Buck was the one who should be afraid. The one thing Spleen couldn't do was stand behind that tree like an idiot when he was no longer sure which side he should be hiding behind; if Buck suspected an ambush he could come round at Spleen from any direction. Spleen decided to head for the slough. Near where the trail ended there was a tree he used to climb. He used to sit up there, watching the blue herons. He would climb the tree, waiting for Buck to come looking for him. The bank was hollowed out there, and Buck would have to lean over, right beneath the tree, to make sure Spleen wasn't hiding down there. Spleen couldn't miss. And if Buck didn't come by he'd stay up in the tree until daylight. Then Buck wouldn't stand a chance. He jogged through the woods parallel to the trail, dodging the trees that loomed at him from the black, trusting that the mayfly din would cover the footfalls that seemed to him louder than shattering glass. The mayfly cloud was getting thicker already; he wasn't sure if it was because he was running or because he was nearing the water or if there were simply more of them – but they were thick as wet snowfall now. The sound, on the other hand, was too loud to get louder, even the water sound, the fish sound, which had reached the decibel level at which is created the illusion that noise is coming from every direction, even though it's only coming from one or two or a long stretch of sloughside. Spleen found the tree, confident that he was well ahead of Buck, if Buck was headed that way at all. The tree was only a few feet from the bank. The water was moiling, dim flashes of silver like frenetic moon reflections on a choppy sea. Above the water the mayflies were a gently swaying curtain in front of Spleen. Closer in they were mayflies, harrassing him with their insidious benevolence. A thick branch at shoulder level curved upwards. Spleen put the gun back into his pants and pulled himself up. He opened his mouth with the effort and a mayfly flew in. He spit it out and climbed further up into the tree. When he was able to sit on a branch facing the water about fifteen feet off the ground he felt safe. The only way Buck would see him before he saw Buck would be if Buck was looking up into every single tree on that end of the Island. He wiped at the mayflies that landed on his face, but soon the bristly hair on his head was alive with them. He ran his hand over his head and felt some of them drop into his shirt. Several mayflies walked on his neck. He had to steady himself on the branch with one hand – soon he might have to have the gun in the other. The mayflies were getting ahead of him. He wiped them off his neck, then his face again, then the top of his head. They were all over his back, dozens inside his shirt. He reached back to shake the shirt, wiggling his back at the same time; still they clung to him. They were back at his neck, walking down his shirt; they were all over his face, on his hair again. He shuddered, ran his hand over his neck, face, and head in one motion. It was getting worse. Maybe the warmth of his body attracted them, or his sweat. Maybe it was just a question of numbers. Having difficulty breathing, he gave up on his back and neck and head, just trying to keep them from his nostrils and eyes. He couldn't tell if he could see the ground anymore, or the water. No flashes of silver were visible, but then it seemed as if the noise was of a different quality now, less fish and more mayfly. He quickly wiped his ears and the old sound came back. He wondered if Buck were being similarly plagued somewhere. He wished there was a way to call it all off and try again the next day. As soon as the first mayfly plugged itself high into his nostril he started down from the tree, having to use both hands climbing, losing his only means of protecting his nose and eyes. By the time he reached the lowest branch he was blind, unable to breathe, forcing himself not to open his mouth, knowing he would only be gulping in mayfies. Spleen hung from the branch a moment and dropped, experiencing another odd rush of suspension when he didn't hit the ground as soon as he thought he would. He had dropped too soon, from the wrong branch; and when he finally landed it was hard; his chin snapped down into his knees and he pitched forward, rolling over once, rising with a stumbling forward momentum, and staggering off the bank, down into a slough of hungry fish.

I prefer to think it's because of what happened next that what happens next a year later is happening, a year later to the day, the hour, the second, the moment hung up between seconds. The mayfly hush has elapsed and the shower of staples inside is louder than outside, a symbolic multitude of brittle tongues flapping. Rita's questionably pubescent, skinny friend has joined her and the drug dealers, sitting right beside the Parasite Lady. They're all suppressing laughter now. The Fag With No Eyebrows has his bag on the table and he's looking in it, and the sound I identify within the din as coming from him is infantile, wheedling. I notice two tables behind him a woman I hope is not familiar. Her back is to me and her hair is brown and I don't want to know if it's her. George and Maynard are talking faster and faster. I can count at least seven people talking to themselves, five women and two men. The raunchy old bitch is hacking, trying to get something across to someone who turns now – it's Lafly Junior, laughing the way he always does, his eyes narrowing a little, looking off into a distance of his own, managing to leave the impression that the air around his face is a bit more rarefied than elsewhere. I don't know what the hell Bette Davis is saying. I look at him and his mouth is moving, and it's not as if I can't hear his voice, but it's coming from somewhere else, mixed in with the laughter of Rita's friends at the other table, with the varied pitch of the various mumblings of schizophrenics, the ascendant anger of George Brown and Maynard, the cascade of raunch falling like bricks off the tongue of that bitch, Lafly's laughter, the Fag's baby talk, all the other voices haggard and scabrous, directionless, fitful, inutile, louder than the aggregation of the entire city's thought and hope and belief in the next sentence, word, syllable, cough, mocking laugh, proposition, excuse, condemnation, so loud I'm compelled to look directly into the maw of silence at two of the only three silences in the joint, the mouth of the Parasite Lady and the little bare ass below that seems immediately to scream for her – a year later, to the second, less than that – a piercing scream (a scream for Spleen) that has horror in it but exceeds horror, anguish and fear but far beneath, from a deeper well of misery and nightmare, a scream at such excruciating pitch that the bag before the

Fag topples and the pigeon inside is loosed, flies straight the other way, away from the scream, crashing through the window, and the Parasite Lady unfazed, the scream unbroken, intensified, and one by one the schizophrenics take it up, each hearing the scream alone and screaming in turn, and George and Maynard stand and begin shouting at them to shut up, the fuck, shut the fuck, up shut the fuck up, turning every direction screaming "Shut up/the fuck up!" and the little ass like the devil's trumpet screaming, Rita screaming,"No no no . . ." They won't get out of her way and she's flailing her arms and screaming, the Fag is at the window crying and screaming, "No no no . . ." He can't see the dead bird now for the mayflies, the mayflies streaming in to the light, the schizophrenics hear the no in their heads telling them no until they want to say yes and therefore no and one by one they're screaming "No no no . . ." Lafly Junior is laughing, looking around and laughing, laughing louder and louder until it reaches the pitch of a scream and he's screaming with the little ass and the Parasite Lady, and Bette Davis claps her hands over her ears and screams like a woman, a real woman, a real scream, and there's that woman, her hair brown, her back to me, and the little ass and the Parasite Lady scream so loud, unbroken, pure as broken glass, that I can't hear the brunette scream, can't hear her stand and scream: "SPLEEN!"

Spleen, surrounded by fish crazed by the inability to swim from their gluttony, lifted himself out of the shallow water. Richie Buck stood before him, annoyed by the mayflies.

The shot was fired.

Spleen made an animal noise.